Also by Ruth Quayle

The Battle of the Blighty Bling

The RACE to HORNSWAGGLE ROCK

Ruth Quayle

ILLUSTRATED BY PHILIP DAVENPORT

ANDERSEN PRESS

First published in Great Britain in 2019 by
Andersen Press Limited
20 Vauxhall Bridge Road
London SW1V 2SA
www.andersenpress.co.uk

2 4 6 8 10 9 7 5 3 1

British Library Cataloguing in Publication Data available.

ISBN 978 1 78344 828 9

Printed and bound in Great Britain by
Clays Ltd, Elcograf S.p.A.

To my sisters,
Tamsin and Anna

CHAPTER 1

My name is Victoria Parrot McScurvy. I'm descended from a long line of pirates. You could say I'm pirate royalty but most people just call me Vic. I live on a ship called *Sixpoint Sally* with my family. According to some people we're a bit of a rabble. We have messy hair and bad manners. We're not your average family.

First of all there's my mum. She is at least six foot three inches, which in case you don't know is very tall for a woman. She wears party dresses with short sleeves to show off all her muscles and tattoos.

And she laughs most of the time – except when she's shouting.

Dad is much smaller than Mum. Mum bosses him around and makes him bail out the bilges. She says Dad is a lazybones.

I share a hammock with my younger brother, Bert. He thinks he is nearly as tall as me but this is just because he stands on tippy-toes. Sharing a hammock with my brother is not very relaxing. This is because Bert is addicted to collecting skimming stones. I tell Bert that skimming stones are not comfy to sleep on but Bert doesn't listen.

Bert and I have quite a lot of fights about his skimming stones. When Bert isn't throwing them, he likes to hide them in an old pillowcase. He thinks this stops me from nicking them but it doesn't. Last week I took his favourite blue skimmer and made it do fifty-seven skims.

You should have heard his screams. Mum says Bert's fuse is even shorter than Dad's legs. They're both crosspatches.

Our very cute – but very naughty – little sister, Maud, doesn't have a hammock. She prefers to sleep up in the crow's nest with just her nuggy for company (Maud's nuggy is a disgusting old blanket that she can't live without). I know that the crow's nest isn't the safest place for a toddler to sleep but Maud screams if Mum and Dad don't let her. Maud has a very loud scream.

Maud likes being up high. She says it's because it's rockier up there and rocking helps her to sleep. But this is just an excuse. Maud doesn't have ANY trouble sleeping. But we're secretly quite glad that Maud doesn't sleep near us.

She's teething, which means she bites everything in sight, including our bottoms. Mum says it's a phase.

Apart from the screaming and biting, Maud is the best sister in the whole world. She is a menace.

You may already have heard of the McScurvys. A few months ago, we won the Battle of the Blighty Bling. It was on the news and everything.

But in case you missed it, here's a quick recap:

Back then our family weren't feeling one bit piratey. We had lost our ship and (nearly) all our treasure and we were living in a rundown caravan on the south coast. Mum and Dad stacked shelves (and stole food) in the local supermarket.

But one day when our mum and dad were at work, we kids (with the help of two non-pirate pals called Arabella and George) took to the high seas, fought off our old arch-enemy Captain Guillemot the Third, won back our long-lost pirate ship, *Sixpoint Sally*, and rescued the Blighty Bling. The Blighty Bling is a famous jewel that acts like a third eye, helping you find a safe way through rocks and whirlpools.

Now we're the most famous pirates in England again. Sort of. Dad says we'll go down in history. Mum says don't count your chickens.

But we don't have any chickens. We just have Pedro, our very grumpy pet parrot. At the moment Pedro is even grumpier than usual. This is because he is lonely. Pedro wants to meet a nice lady parrot to grow old with. But parrots are rare on the south coast of England. The only birds around here are seagulls and pigeons and they're not Pedro's type.

Mum says Pedro is lovesick. I asked Mum what being lovesick feels like but she laughed and said 'Chance would be a fine thing', which made Dad even grumpier than usual.

We used to wear shoes and do homework. But now we've got our ship back, we live it up on the high seas. We sing shanties till dawn. We count our treasure. We sail around looking for trouble. We sleep in till late. Then we just get up, chew a bit of bubblegum, have a splash about in the sea and mooch around till lunch. No one tells us what to do. If we're naughty our parents pat us on our backs.

At least they USED TO. Recently, though, things have changed. Or, rather, our mum has.

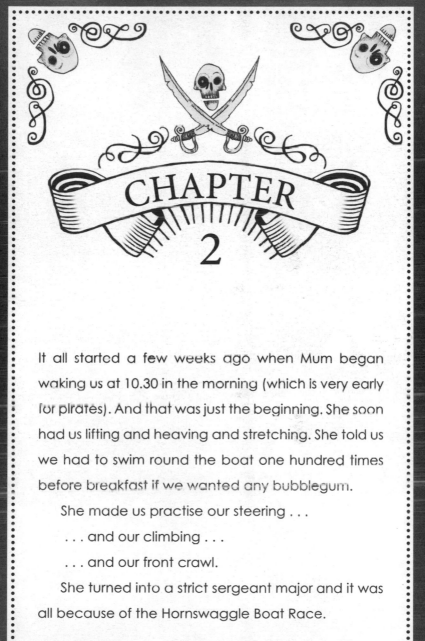

CHAPTER

2

It all started a few weeks ago when Mum began waking us at 10.30 in the morning (which is very early for pirates). And that was just the beginning. She soon had us lifting and heaving and stretching. She told us we had to swim round the boat one hundred times before breakfast if we wanted any bubblegum.

She made us practise our steering . . .

. . . and our climbing . . .

. . . and our front crawl.

She turned into a strict sergeant major and it was all because of the Hornswaggle Boat Race.

The Hornswaggle Boat Race takes place every four years and is the most important event in the pirate calendar. It starts in a town called Shabbers-on-Sea and finishes ten miles out to sea at – you guessed it – Hornswaggle Rock.

Hundreds of ships have been wrecked on Hornswaggle Rock over the years. It's an enormous piece of granite in the shape of a rhino's horn. But you can only see the rock at low tide. Once the tide comes up, it disappears under the sea. Mum says the tide waits for no pirate. In other words, if you take your time, Hornswaggle Rock won't be there when you arrive.

To get to the rock you have to sail through treacherous seas stuffed with sharks. And even if you manage to survive the sharks, you have to end the race by sailing up Shipwreck Strait, a narrow gully that runs between two rocky islands. Shipwreck Strait is famous for its dangerous tides and currents. Mum says one wrong move and you're a goner. Dad says any chance of a quiet life.

To win the race, you have to be the first crew to

grab the flag from the tip of Hornswaggle Rock and bring it back to Shabbers-on-Sea.

There is only one rule in the Hornswaggle Boat Race: you have to sail the whole thing. You're not allowed to row, or use an engine, or take a shortcut. Apart from that you can cheat as much as you like. Dad says the skill is in the cheating. But he would say this because he's not very good at steering. There are no prizes for coming second or third or fourth. You either win or you lose.

We mostly lose.

Non-pirates think the Hornswaggle is an ordinary sailing competition run by the Royal Hornswaggle Yacht Club. They don't realise that it's a pirate race and that the Hornswaggle Yacht Club's chairwoman, Dame Kittiwake, is a tough and dastardly pirate.

They HAVE NO IDEA they're actually racing against the UK's five biggest pirate crews – the McScurvys (that's us), the Guillemots (our worst enemies), the Rattle-Dazzlers from Scotland, the Swiggers from Cornwall and the O'Drearys from Skegness.

The Swiggers won the first Hornswaggle in 1922 but Dame Kittiwake holds the record for the most races won by one crew. She's won it seven times and she was single-handed too – without a crew. Since she retired, no Kittiwakes have dared take part.

Each time, the race is dirtier and more cutthroat than the last. That's because all pirates are desperate to get their hands on the famous Hornswaggle trophy . . . A.K.A. the Treasurescope.

The Treasurescope looks like a golden telescope. But don't be fooled. Hidden in its lens are hundreds of rare and valuable treasure maps. In other words, if you win the Hornswaggle Boat Race, you have a head start on finding all the hidden pirate treasure in the world. Mum says the Treasurescope is like the best treasure map you've never had – multiplied by a trillion.

You're probably wondering why any pirate would agree to give back the Treasurescope at the end of the four years. But we don't really have a choice. Any pirate who refuses to return the Treasurescope gets a personal visit from Dame Kittiwake. And, believe me, Dame Kittiwake is as tough as old whale bone.

Mum says that when Guillemot the Third ran off with the Treasurescope twelve years ago (before any of us kids were even born) Dame Kittiwake tracked him down in Costa Rica and threatened to shave off his eyebrows. He handed it over straight away.

The last McScurvy to win the Treasurescope was our grandfather Stan back in 1984. Then he spent four years sailing the world and he found loads of valuable treasure.

But since Stan's day things haven't gone so well for the McScurvys. So you can see why Mum really, really wants to win this year. She says there's no point sailing the seas looking for treasure if we don't even know where to start. She says it's about time we lived up to the McScurvy name.

The problem is the other pirate crews want the Treasurescope just as much as we do. And . . . they're better at winning. The Rattle-Dazzlers are enormous and strong, the Swiggers have the fastest ship in existence and the O'Drearys outnumber everybody else (they have NINE children). As for Captain Guillemot, well he's just really good at cheating.

Luckily Captain Guillemot couldn't enter this year's race because he doesn't have a ship. His ship, *The Raven*, sank on the Hammerhead Rocks a few months ago during the Battle of the Blighty Bling. Since then Captain Guillemot has been living in a spa hotel on the mainland. Mum says he's addicted to beauty treatments. This was good news for us. Because with Guillemot out of action, we had one less crew to beat.

Unfortunately our mum is not a very good coach. She shouts too much. She makes us scrub the decks for hours if we don't practise our front crawl (the Hornswaggle Boat Race always ends with a swim for the flag). She even made Bert walk the plank for not digging in his heels in when he was climbing the mast. Mum says our pirate pride depends on us winning. And she screams like a sick parrot when we muck around during training sessions. She is very competitive.

For instance, today (the morning of the race), she woke us at 4.30 a.m. She said we needed plenty of time to get to Shabbers-on-Sea for the start of the race at midday. She told us

to feel the air filling our lungs. We mostly just felt sleepy.

But we perked up a few hours later when we reached the Bay of Barnacles. The Bay of Barnacles is a stretch of water close to where we used to live in our old caravan. Whenever we sail back here, it feels a bit like we're going home.

The sun rose over the horizon. It left streaks like orange-ripple ice cream across the sky. Maud said it was a tasty-looking sky and we agreed.

By 8 a.m. we actually began to feel quite jolly. But then things started to go wrong.

It was all Dad's fault for forgetting to go to the supermarket.

CHAPTER
3

When Bert is hungry, he is even more annoying than usual. He shouts things like 'I'm going to die if I don't eat!' and 'My tummy hurts' and 'Give me food'. He starts to wail and whinge and stamp his feet. When Bert is hungry he is not nice to be around.

Once, we had to skip lunch because we were being chased by a man in a speedboat, and Bert had a tantrum for two and a half hours. It was a McScurvy record – and that's saying something.

None of us likes having an empty stomach. When Mum is hungry, she starts to shout. When Dad is hungry he storms off in a sulk. When Maud is hungry she bites even more than usual. When I'm hungry, I burp. Loudly.

So when Bert announced at 8.06 a.m. this morning that he needed to eat RIGHT NOW OR ELSE, we weren't surprised one bit. We were hungry too. All we'd had to eat since 4.30 a.m. was half a piece of bubblegum and a sip of lemonade.

'Where are the pains au chocolat?' asked Dad. Dad loves French food.

'I could murder a bacon sandwich,' said Mum.

Mum and Dad climbed down to the galley to get breakfast while we stayed on deck, steering the ship. My mouth was watering as I got ready to feast on salt and vinegar chipsticks and chocolate fingers.

We're allowed to eat whatever we like as long as it's unhealthy. Mum doesn't believe in fruit and veg. She says you can't trust food that's covered in mud. My sister Maud eats only one thing – strawberry sherbets. She once tried a fish-finger sandwich but she spat it straight into the sea. She said it tasted of goldfish poo.

Maud crunched her last strawberry sherbet and started looking around for something else to chew on.

'Breakfast is coming, Maud,' I told her. 'Won't be long.'

But when Mum and Dad poked their heads out of the cabin they weren't holding any strawberry sherbets. They weren't holding any bags of salt and vinegar chipsticks. They didn't have any chocolate fingers. And they weren't smiling.

'Do you want the good news or the bad news?' asked Mum.

Bert looked at them crossly. 'We just want breakfast.'

Dad scratched his head. 'The bad news is that I forgot to go to the supermarket to do the stealing.' (Stealing is a pirate version of shopping. It's perfectly normal.)

'ARGH!'

Maud bit Bert's arm. Bert shouted at the top of his voice. I burped.

'But the good news,' said Mum cheerfully, 'is that we don't need to be in Shabbers-on-Sea for ages. Which means . . . ' She grinned at us all. 'There's plenty of time for a supermarket raid!'

We cheered. This *was* good news. Supermarket raids are even better than fridge raids. There's way more choice and we get to do trolley races up and down the aisles. Trolley races are our second-best thing after stealing. Once Bert managed to get up to 30 m.p.h. on the frozen-food aisle. He had to crash land in the ice-cream section but that didn't matter. He nicked us all a choc ice.

Mum and Dad often make us kids do the supermarket raids. They say it's because we are less suspicious-looking than them. But we know it's just because they're too lazy. We don't mind though. We love going ashore and we love a raid.

Mum steered *Sixpoint Sally* through the Bay of Barnacles' dangerous whirlpools and turned towards Blipstow, which is the name of the tatty seaside town where we used to live. Bert picked up his pillowcase full of skimming stones and staggered on to the deck.

'If you think I'm leaving these behind, unguarded,' he muttered, 'you're wrong.'

I ignored him. I was too busy looking out for our favourite beach. It's always our first stop when we visit the mainland. We like to sit on the breakwaters and see who can spot the best bit of rubbish floating on the water. We never get bored of it.

When we first arrive, Maud always shouts rude words out to sea. Once a lady with a dog told Mum that Maud had bad manners. Mum shook the lady's hand and said, 'Thank you, what a lovely thing to say.' Because if you're a pirate, having bad manners is a good thing. Then Mum told the lady that she might want to keep an eye on her dog because he was doing a poo in somebody's beach bag and that wasn't particularly good manners was it? The lady went bright red. She didn't bother us after that.

Sometimes we go and see Granny McScurvy on her houseboat. She has moved to Blipstow from the Thames. She says it's to spend more time with us but really it's because she's addicted to the beach-front arcade games. Granny McScurvy knows all the latest pirate news. Plus, she has a really big telly.

And we always ALWAYS fit in a visit to Arabella and George. Arabella and George are our best pals. They're the ones who helped us win the Battle of the Blighty Bling. They aren't actually pirates but Mum says they're honorary McScurvys, and that's a fact.

Arabella has grand ambitions. She says life in a rundown seaside town is low on excitement. But, the thing is, it isn't.

Not when we're around.

CHAPTER 4

Bert, Maud and I rowed ashore while Mum and Dad stayed on board for a crashout. A crashout is a pirate version of a nap. When pirates are having a crashout it's almost impossible to wake them.

Which is why we left Pedro as a lookout while Mum and Dad slept. We knew that no one would want to climb aboard with Pedro there. Pedro has a very sharp beak.

'Don't be long,' Mum shouted. 'We've got a race to win. So we definitely can't risk anyone spotting *Sixpoint Sally* and reporting her to the police.'

People round here are suspicious of pirate ships.

Luckily the beach was deserted. We tied our rowing boat to a large rock and headed into town. On the way to the supermarket, we passed Arabella and George's house, which is nothing like our pirate ship. For a start, it is painted white with blue window frames. There's also a neat and tidy lawn and a bush that's clipped in the shape of a cat. Arabella says her dad trims it every weekend.

Arabella and George's dad is not very keen on us. He thinks we're scruffy layabouts who shouldn't go anywhere near his nice, clean, well-brought-up children. But Arabella is cleverer than her dad. She explains to him that it is very good for her and George to mix with different types of people for a change. She tells him we're her civic duty and she'll get a Blue Peter badge for it.

Arabella's dad says, 'Well that's very noble of you, Arabella. I'm proud of you.' And Arabella winks at us.

Arabella's mum is not around much. In fact, we've never even met her. This is because she has an important job. Arabella says it is in an office and, like most things round here, it is very boring.

We peered through the windows but there was nobody home.

'They must be at school,' I said.

Maud stamped her feet. She shouted 'Bum' and bit the doorknob. 'Bum' is Maud's new favourite word. She says it when she's happy or sad or cross. She says it a lot. Right now she was cross because George wasn't there. George is Maud's favourite person in the whole world. George is the only person Maud doesn't bite.

'BUM!'

'Come on, Maud,' I told her. 'You'll see George soon. Let's get to the supermarket and I'll let you nick a bumper jar of strawberry sherbets.'

Maud cheered up at once.

Luckily the supermarket was fairly empty. There were just a few old people with shopping trolleys and the odd mum or dad with a buggy. This was good news for us because trolley races are way trickier when a supermarket is busy.

'We've got five minutes,' I told the others. 'Grab what you can, fill your trolley and run for it.'

Then I called after them and said, 'Don't get greedy, don't get caught,' because this is our family motto.

The problem is, we're not very good at sticking to it. We're nearly always greedy and we usually get caught. Mum says there's nothing wrong with good clean stealing. But normal people don't agree with her. They think money makes the world go round.

We're not totally bad, though. We only really steal from other pirates and the biggest supermarkets. For smaller shops like this one, we always carry a few bits of gold with us. We like to leave a nugget or two on the counter on our way out – sometimes more depending on the size of our raid.

Most of the time, the cashiers like the gold so much they forget to call the police. This makes it a win-win situation. But right now, all we could think about was breakfast. Bert and I grabbed a trolley and raced straight to the crisps. Maud skipped over to the sweets.

Five minutes is not long to get enough food to last the whole of the Hornswaggle Boat Race. We threw in bags of crisps and chocolate bars. We grabbed every jar of strawberry sherbets in the shop. We piled in lollipops and bubblegum balls and marshmallows and frozen yoghurts. We shoved in five bottles of Coke and lemonade. We stopped when the trolley was full to the brim.

'Time for a quick drive?' said Bert. I grinned and nodded. Bert and I set off at a run and leaped on to our overflowing trolley. We whizzed past the baked beans. We flew past the washing powder. We went so fast the supermarket shelves became a blur. We must have been going at around 20 m.p.h. when . . .

. . . we crashed into the tinned tuna.

There was a loud smashing sound as tins and jars toppled to the floor. I flew through the air and

landed on top of a pile of pasta. Bert hurtled in the opposite direction and landed head first in an old lady's trolley. Our food spilled out everywhere.

Customers came running out of the aisles.

'Hooligans,' said the old lady. 'He's squished my malt loaf.'

'Sorry about that,' I muttered, pulling Bert out of the trolley.

Saying sorry doesn't come naturally to me but Arabella says it's a good way of getting out of trouble. This time though sorry didn't seem to be helping. The customers and the cashier were not happy at all. Bert and I grabbed our food and piled it back into the trolley. We had to get out of here before the cashier called the police.

'Maud!' shouted Bert. 'Put your tongue away and come and help us.'

I glanced at Maud and my heart sank. Now they would definitely call the police. Stealing is one thing, spoiling the food for other customers is worse. And Maud was definitely spoiling the food. She was biting her way through every packet of sweets on the shelf. If she didn't like a particular sweet, she popped it back into the packet, half-eaten, and moved on to the next one. She didn't seem to care that a group of shoppers were watching her with their mouths wide open.

She just gave them a sticky grin and waved. ''Ello, funny people!' she said happily. 'We're doing a raid.'

'Maud, shhhhh,' hissed Bert. 'Raids are against the law.'

I picked Maud up and popped her in the trolley. She threw a sweet at me so I ducked. The sweet flew through the air and stuck to Bert's head. But Bert didn't even notice. He was busy trying to heave his pillowcase full of skimming stones into the trolley alongside Maud.

'I told you not to bother bringing those stupid stones,' I said.

'I told you to mind your own business.'

'No you didn't.'

'Well I'm telling you now. Mind your own business. An' they're not stupid, they're useful and interesting.'

'Fine,' I said. 'If you want to lug old stones around everywhere you go, you're welcome to it. I've got slightly bigger things to worry about.'

'Oh yes,' said Bert in his most annoying and most sarcastic voice. 'Like what?'

'Like getting out of this supermarket before the police arrive.'

'Right,' muttered Bert. 'Good point.' He heaved his pillowcase into the trolley and grabbed the handle.

'Ready?' I said.

'Ready.'

I found a gold nugget in my pocket and flung it at the cashier. Then we ran for it. We were through the automatic doors before I could say 'Shiver my timbers'. The fresh air hit our faces and excitement fizzed through our blood like Coca-Cola in an icy glass. **'Yeeeee haaaaaa!'** shouted Bert as the trolley trundled across the cobbles.

'Bum!' shrieked Maud, as an unopened packet of sweets flew into the road.

Trolleys aren't the most stable things at the best of times. When they're full of junk food, they're even more wobbly than Mum's belly – and way heavier. They're not very fast either. Behind us, I could hear the shop's security guard. He was grunting and puffing and getting closer with each stride.

'Hold on tight!' I told the others, yanking the trolley into a side alley lined with rubbish bins. 'I know a shortcut!'

I promise I'm not exaggerating when I say that me, Bert and Maud know the nooks and crannies of this seaside town better than anyone. It's because we're so used to getting chased by security guards.

The narrow side alley led into a busy boat yard.

From here, we hid behind rusty boat engines and old anchors and quickly made our way down to the beach.

After a few minutes, Bert started to laugh.

'We've lost him!' he said, pointing. 'Look!'

The security guard was lumbering up the hill, towards the campsite on the outskirts of the town.

Maud and I laughed back. There's nothing like a supermarket raid to get you in a good mood. Nearly getting caught just makes it more exciting. Plus, the sun was shining and there was a gentle sea breeze. We stopped briefly to eat some salt and vinegar chipsticks, chocolate fingers and bubblegum (we

still hadn't eaten breakfast after all).

I grinned at the others.

'In this weather, we'll be able to sail to Shabbers-on-Sea in no time.'

Bert and Maud cheered and blew pink bubbles. For just a moment, everything seemed to be going our way. Soon we'd be rowing back out to our pirate ship and on our way to the start of the race.

But when we got back to the beach, we stopped laughing and we stopped skipping too. Bert's pink bubble burst all over his face.

'Bum,' said Maud. 'Bum, bum, bum.'

Our rowing boat wasn't tied up to the rock where we'd left it.

It was in the sea.

And it was full of people.

CHAPTER
5

At first glance I thought they were ghosts. They were all dressed in floaty white things and they seemed to be swaying in the breeze.

'Schpooky,' said Maud, biting hard on a strawberry sherbet.

'Very spooky,' agreed Bert, pulling a stone out of his pillowcase and skimming it into the sea towards our rowing boat.

The stone hit the boat and the ghosts looked up. I squinted to get a closer look. My heart sank.

'They're not ghosts,' I said gloomily. 'They're something a lot worse.'

In our boat were three men and one woman and the reason I'd thought they were ghosts is because they were all wearing white fluffy bathrobes. But I knew exactly who they were. Captain Guillemot the Third, our oldest archest enemy, and his pirate crew, Beefster, Cath and Bones.

We hadn't seen them for months, not since *The Raven* went down on the Hammerhead Rocks. Not since we'd stolen back the Blighty Bling and ruined Guillemot's best jacket. Which did not go down well.

Captain Guillemot is the vainest pirate on the south coast. He goes to all the fashion shows and is known as the Hipster Ripster. But don't get taken in by the fancy clothes. Captain Guillemot is evil and nasty. He's even more competitive than our mum.

He'd had his hair dyed since we'd last seen him. It was blacker than ever and it was pulled back into an elaborate bun. He was wearing dangly diamond earrings, a silk bandana and a huge pair of sunglasses. He laughed and waved.

'He's meant to be staying in a spa hotel,' said

Bert. 'That's what you told me.'

'That's what Mum and Dad told me,' I snapped. 'And by the look of those white bathrobes and his new hairdo, he probably was staying in a spa hotel. But one thing's for sure, he isn't now. He's in our rowing boat.'

'What do you think he's up to?'

'I don't *think*, I *know*. He hasn't got a ship of his own, so he's going to try and steal our ship so he can win the Hornswaggle Boat Race. Look! He's rowing out to *Sixpoint Sally*.'

Bert grabbed a bottle of tomato ketchup from our trolley and lobbed it at Captain Guillemot's head. But Captain Guillemot was rowing quickly. Not even Bert could throw that far. The tomato ketchup landed in the water with a big splash.

Captain Guillemot laughed. So did Beefster, Cath and Bones.

'Nice throw!' he shouted.

'I'd like to see you get past Pedro,' replied Bert. 'Go on, just try!'

'Meanie!' screeched Maud. 'Nasty, horrid, sluggy,

slimy, meanie, moany man with yellow teeth and, and –' Maud paused to think of a really bad insult – 'and wrinkles!' she announced triumphantly.

I was about to tell Maud that, for the millionth time, Guillemot's teeth weren't yellow they were gold and that he was even more of a biter than she is, when Guillemot stopped rowing.

'FYI,' he said, thrusting his face towards us. 'I don't have one single wrinkle any more. Not since my aqua hydrating UV injection therapy. Even my hands are smooth. Look!'

I have to admit his bronzed skin did look very soft and *very* smooth.

'You can't take our boat,' I told him. 'We're on our way to Shabbers-on-Sea and we're taking part in the Hornswaggle Boat Race.'

'Correction,' said Guillemot nastily. '*I'm* taking part in the Hornswaggle Boat Race. You didn't think I was going to let the small matter of not having a pirate ship stop me from getting my hands on the Treasurescope did you?'

He picked up the oars and started rowing towards our ship.

'Pedro!' I hollered. 'Get your beak out. GET READY FOR BATTLE!'

I knew we could rely on Pedro. After all he is the best guard bird in the world. On my sixth birthday, we left him in charge of our ship when we came ashore for pizza. While we were stuffing our faces in Da Marios, the Swiggers sailed up from Cornwall and tried to break in to *Sixpoint Sally* to steal our treasure. Pedro scared them away with one very sharp peck. Since then, we've always left him in charge of our ship when we're not there.

Pedro is way better than an alarm or CCTV. He's scarier than an angry Rottweiler. Pirates do not mess with Pedro. They take one look at that beak and run (well, row) for it. But Captain Guillemot was not like most pirates.

'I must say,' he said, sneering, 'that parrot of yours is the scariest thing I've ever seen. I mean just look at him.'

Captain Guillemot has a way with sarcasm. But if I'm honest (which I'm not very often) I knew what he meant. Pedro didn't look very scary. He was sitting on the prow of *Sixpoint Sally* but he wasn't doing any of the things a good guard bird is supposed to do. He wasn't squawking or spitting or pointing his beak. He wasn't sharpening his claws. He was gazing dreamily at something in Captain Guillemot's boat.

I peered a bit more closely to see what it was that Pedro had spotted. Was it a gold necklace? Was it something chocolatey? Was it a ripe banana?

It wasn't any of these things. The thing that Pedro was gazing at was sitting on Captain Guillemot's shoulder. It had pink and green feathers and a perky purple crest. It was the prettiest parrot I had ever seen.

'Go for it, Pamela,' Guillemot laughed. 'Show that grumpy old guard parrot what a pretty Polly you are.'

Remember what I said about Pedro looking for love and not being himself at the moment? Well all I can say is we should have thought about this *before* we went off to do our supermarket raid. We should have remembered that on the morning of the Hornswaggle Boat Race, other pirates will do *anything* they can to make sure they win. Especially if they don't have a ship of their own to race in.

We should have remembered that even though Captain Guillemot was living in a spa hotel on the mainland, getting his hair dyed and enjoying a full range of beauty treatments, he was still a pirate. And he was still our old arch-enemy. We should have remembered that it takes more than a lovesick parrot to frighten Captain Guillemot.

Bert stopped trying to throw things. Maud stopped grinding her teeth. For a moment all we could do was stare. Guillemot's pink and green parrot lifted her purple-crested head. She glanced at Pedro and looked up at him with large, shining, beady eyes. She flapped a wing.

Pedro gave a loud squawk. Then he fell off his perch and plummeted into the sea.

Captain Guillemot took his chance. He rowed quickly to the ladder that hung over *Sixpoint Sally*'s stern. Right on cue, Pamela flew up into the air and did a little double-twist back flip in the sky. Then she flew away. Pedro heaved himself out of the sea and shook the water off his feathers. He didn't even glance at Captain Guillemot and the other pirates. He flew after Pamela. Soon the two parrots were just specks in the distance.

Guillemot climbed up the rope ladder on to our ship.

'Facials and manicures are fine for a bit,' he shouted, laughing nastily. 'But you can't beat a life at sea – even on a rust-bucket of a ship like this.'

Captain Guillemot put his smooth manicured hands on *Sixpoint Sally*'s ship's wheel and laughed.

Come on, Mum and Dad, I thought. For prawn's sake, wake up and stop him. But Mum and Dad were mid-crashout. I could almost hear their snores. They wouldn't wake for ages.

Beefster hauled up *Sixpoint Sally*'s anchor.

'I'd love to stay and chat,' hollered Guillemot. 'But I need to get myself to Shabbers-on-Sea. I have a Treasurescope to win. Tell Pamela I said goodbye. If you see her again, that is!'

Captain Guillemot laughed some more. Then he hoisted the mainsail and steered *Sixpoint Sally* out of the Bay of Barnacles.

I couldn't believe it. We'd only just rescued our old pirate ship and now we'd gone and lost her again. Worse than that, we'd lost her on the morning of the most important event in the pirate calendar. And our mum and dad were still on board.

I tried not to think about what Guillemot might start doing to them. Most pirates would never attack another pirate while they're sleeping but Guillemot doesn't give two bellows about doing the decent thing. He'd have no worries about throwing our parents overboard mid-crashout. We HAD to do something.

But what? We were standing on a beach miles from Shabbers-on-Sea and all we had was a pillowcase full of stupid skimming stones and a supermarket trolley full of junk food. Anyone could see our situation was not exactly hearty. Anyone could see we were the unluckiest pirates on the planet.

'Come on,' I shouted to the others. 'Hurry!'

I grabbed our trolley and started pushing it back towards town. Bert and Maud stared after me, then they started to follow.

'Where are we going?' demanded Bert.

'School,' I replied. 'That's where!'

CHAPTER

6

The local school was at the top of a windy hill. Its concrete buildings were the same colour as a pair of white pants that have gone grey in the wash. The only bit of colour was the football pitch but you couldn't really see much green because it was covered in faded crisp packets and sodden school jumpers. School was the ugliest place in the world. Even Bert and I agreed about this.

We couldn't squeeze our shopping trolley through the gap in the fence so we left it where it was, grabbed our favourite bits of food and shoved them into our pockets. Bert heaved his pillowcase on to his back and we pushed our way through. We crouched behind an overflowing rubbish bin next to the main assembly hall.

The door of the hall was open and the air that wafted out smelled of school dinners, sweaty trainers and floor polish.

'School makes me feel sick,' said Bert.

'Sicky Bert,' said Maud happily. 'Bert's a sicky boy.'

'Aim for the bin,' I said.

'Stop being so bossy,' Bert gasped.

Maud bit his arm.

'I'll puke on you if you're not careful,' Bert told her crossly, heaving into the bin.

'Shhhhhh!' I told them. 'Listen.'

Inside the hall a teacher was telling a class to do twenty star jumps. Maud took her nuggy out of her mouth.

'I'm gonna fight that meanie teacher,' she said, making fists with her hands.

Maud does not like teachers. This is mainly

because teachers do not like Maud. When we were still living in our wobbly old caravan, Maud tried pre-school for a few weeks. At first it was OK. Everyone said 'Ooh' and 'Ah' and 'Isn't she adorable'. Because my sister is very cute. But then Maud kept making the teachers cry. She stole Mrs Harris's gold earrings. She drew treasure maps all over the picture books. She taught the other children to shout 'Poo-poo bum' during story time.

The teachers sent hundreds of cross letters home about Maud. Mum and Dad took Maud for an ice-cream sundae to celebrate.

School was the worst thing that ever happened to us. We had to learn things like how to divide fractions. We had to write about what we did at the weekend in our neatest handwriting. We had to play *netball* for prawn's sake – and we weren't even allowed to cheat.

Personally, I don't see how knowing the answer to 12 x 9 will help you sail the seas or win the Treasurescope. But right now we couldn't risk getting into a fight with a teacher. I shook my head.

'No fighting, Maud. The teachers will just catch us and make us sit on the carpet and do literacy. You don't want that again, do you?'

Bert stopped retching over the bin.

'Well why *are* we here then?'

'Haven't you guessed yet?'

'No, that's why I'm asking.'

Sometimes, well quite a lot really, I wish my brother was just a teensy bit clever. I sighed.

'Who do we know who goes to this school?'

Bert scowled and narrowed his eyes. He spent a

long time scratching his head. Then he looked up.

'Oh,' he said, smiling.

'Exactly,' I said. 'And right now, Arabella and George are our only hope.'

A bell rang loudly. Children raced out of the classrooms into the playground. Soon there were children screaming and running in every direction.

'Come on,' I told the others, setting off towards the playground. 'It's morning break. Arabella and George are sure to be here somewhere.'

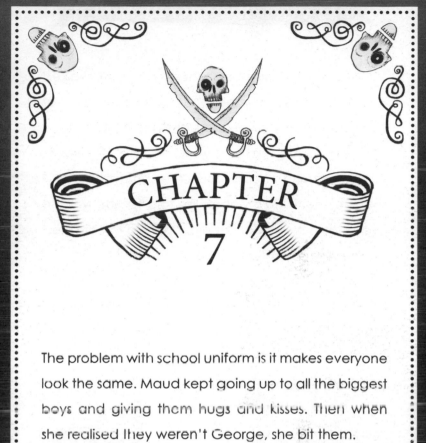

CHAPTER

7

The problem with school uniform is it makes everyone look the same. Maud kept going up to all the biggest boys and giving them hugs and kisses. Then when she realised they weren't George, she bit them.

Now, even I know that this is not normal playground behaviour. Schools aren't used to children like Maud. A boy with black hair and a smug face kept looking at us and whispering. He headed in our direction.

Bert turned to me.

'I think we'd better leave.'

I nodded and grabbed Maud's hand. We walked quickly towards the gap in the fence. But Maud sat down, refused to move and started to wail loudly.

'I want George!' she shouted. 'Where's George?'

Bert promised her his favourite skimming stone. I said she could bite my nose. We told her she was the best sister in the world. But Maud would not budge.

The boy caught up with us.

'I'm telling on you,' he said. 'I'm going to tell a teacher you're trespassing on school property. I'm going to tell a teacher that you're carrying weapons and that you're eating bubblegum. I'm going to get you in BIG TROUBLE. I'm going to . . .'

A shadow fell across the ground in front of us.

'Good morning,' said a woman in a deep voice. 'What's the problem?'

The woman was very small. She was wearing a long skirt, a large hat and a pair of glasses perched at the end of her nose.

The boy blinked. 'Who are you?' he asked.

'Thank you so much, Sam Thornton,' said the woman in an even deeper voice. 'I'll deal with this now. Off you trot.'

The boy paused for a minute. He still looked puzzled.

'Begone!' said the woman, her deep voice echoing round the whole playground.

Sam Thornton walked away, kicking his feet as he went and glancing behind him. We stood looking at this scary teacher woman in old-fashioned clothes.

Was she going to take us inside and make us do algebra? Was she going to send us to the head? Was she going to call the police?

'Bye then,' I said, trying to sound as though we'd just accidentally wandered into school by mistake. 'We're just leaving.' I walked towards the gap in the fence.

'Not so fast!' said the woman, grabbing me by the shoulder.

Then she burst out laughing.

'George!' She shouted at a large boy giving piggyback rides to some of the smaller children. 'Come here!'

George wandered over. He looked different in his school uniform, sort of older and younger at the same time. He still had the same knitted hat and staring eyes, though. He was holding a bag that seemed to be full of scraps of material.

Maud leaped into his arms and nibbled his nose.

'George,' I whispered. 'Where's Arabella?'

The woman laughed again.

'Yes, George, *where's* Arabella?!' she said.

George didn't say anything (he never says much).
He just smiled at Maud.

'I'm glad you appreciate my acting skills,' said the
woman. 'I think it's because I like to get so involved in
a role. I'm a fan of the Stanislavski school of acting.
You have to immerse yourself in the character, you
have to live and breathe your part, you have to
BECOME the person you are playing.'

The woman stopped speaking for a moment and
smirked. She took off her glasses and winked at us.

'Arabella?' I whispered.

'I'm playing a suffragette in our school play, which I wrote myself. We're in the middle of rehearsals at the moment. George is making all the costumes. He's never without a needle these days. He can sew anything. Mrs Nichols says he should set his sights on a career in fashion. Anyway . . .' Arabella paused. 'What are you lot doing at school?'

'It's a long story.' I sighed.

'Give us the short version then,' said Arabella, glancing at her watch.

So we told them about the Hornswaggle Boat Race and the Treasurescope. We told them about coming ashore to get food, about our supermarket raid and about Pedro flying off into the distance with a parrot called Pamela. We told them about Captain Guillemot stealing *Sixpoint Sally* with our parents on board.

'So you see,' I finished. 'We really need to get to Shabbers-on-Sea before the race starts at midday, and we need to rescue Mum and Dad too, but we don't have a boat.'

I paused. I knew the next part of my plan was a bit of a risk.

'I was wondering if we could borrow your dad's boat again? We'll look after it really well. We promise.'

Arabella laughed and went back to her grand acting voice.

'I think we all know that a pirate promise isn't worth diddly squid,' she said.

I'd forgotten how annoying Arabella could be.

'Anyway,' she continued. 'It's a no-go. Dad sold his boat last month. He spent the money on a new ride-on lawnmower.'

My heart sank. Our dream of rescuing Mum and Dad and trying to win the Hornswaggle Boat Race was rapidly slipping further away. The school bell rang. Breaktime was over. Now Arabella and George would have to go back to lessons and we'd be on our own once again. With no boat, no plan, no parents and not even a tiny grain of hope.

I looked at the grey buildings and realised that without our pirate ship and treasure we'd be forced to move back to our leaky caravan. Mum and Dad would have to go back to working (well, stealing) in the supermarket – that's if they weren't dead. And we'd have to go back to school. Our pirate life was over.

'Anyway,' said Arabella, 'even if we did have Dad's boat it would take us far too long to get to Shabbers-on-Sea. We'd never be able catch up with a huge ship like *Sixpoint Sally*.'

'Thanks,' I said crossly. 'You've certainly made us feel A LOT better about things. I'm so glad we came to you for help.'

Arabella snorted.

'Oh honestly,' she said. 'The problem with you pirates is that you never think outside the box. You're so narrow-minded – or should I say narrow-boat-minded – ha ha ha! What I mean is, all you think of is boats, boats, boats. You've got sails and anchors on the brain. Well, my hearties, I have news for you. Sometimes, just sometimes, there are other ways of getting from A to B.'

Arabella grinned. She pushed her glasses back up her nose and pulled down her hat. She gathered up her long skirt. She let out her most piratey laugh.

'Well,' she said. 'Are you with me or not?'

CHAPTER

8

Granny McScurvy is always telling us you don't actually have to be bad to be a good pirate. She's been saying it over since we were babies. Normally we burst out laughing. Because everyone knows that the best pirates are ALWAYS bad. But for the first time in my life I was beginning to see what Granny McScurvy meant. Sometimes a total goody-goody can be properly dastardly.

Take Arabella for instance. She is the goodest person we know. She is head girl of her school, she's house captain, she's the school librarian AND the lunch monitor. Arabella is Keen with a capital K. She's also a mighty fine pirate.

This is partly because she is so brainy. But it's also because she gets away with things that most children can only dream of. It's what makes her so cutthroat. For example, at school, she gets to wear a special Prefect badge pinned to her blazer, she's allowed to walk home on her own, she's on first-name terms with her teachers and, best of all . . .

. . . she has her own set of keys to the school store cupboard. She jangled them in front of us.

'Stay here and keep watch.' She grinned. 'I'll be back in a minute.'

George was the lookout while Bert, Maud and I ducked down behind the bin. In the old days when we went to school, Bert and I always hid in the playground at the end of break. We liked to try to sneak out in our lunch hour to do a supermarket raid. The problem was, we always got caught. Turns out that teachers are just as sneaky as pirates. They have eyes in the backs of their heads.

So I was very relieved when I saw Arabella running

back to join us. And I was especially pleased to see she was grinning.

'Run to the car park!' she hissed, sprinting past us. 'Hurry!'

George put Maud on his shoulders, Bert and I grabbed his pillowcase and we all set off after Arabella. Moving wasn't easy with our pockets full of junk food but anything was better than waiting by that smelly bin.

'Duck down!' said Arabella.

We were passing a classroom window. Arabella got on her hands and knees and crawled along the ground. We all copied. Arabella may not LOOK like a pirate and she may not SOUND like one either. And she may be REALLY, REALLY annoying and she's *definitely* a goody-goody. But, the thing is, when she tells you to do something, it's best just to do it.

I peeped through the classroom window and saw a teacher writing things on a whiteboard while bored children picked their noses and rolled their eyes.

'That'll be us if we don't manage to get *Sixpoint Sally* back,' Bert said, staggering under his pillowcase full of stones and pockets full of cans of Coke.

I wondered if Guillemot had found Mum and Dad. What if he'd thrown them overboard? I knew they'd never be able to survive the deadly whirlpools in the Bay of Barnacles. Dad's front crawl has seen better days. If only Pedro hadn't flown off after Pamela, we could have tied a message to his foot and sent him to Granny McScurvy. Then she could have organised a search party.

'Jolly well stop dallying,' Arabella said. 'Do you want us to get caught?'

'Oh yes,' said Bert crossly. 'That's exactly what we're hoping for.'

I told Bert to put a sock in it, which is pirate for shut up.

'Don't worry,' said Arabella. 'I'm a quick-thinker, if we get caught I'll come up with something.'

Bert rolled his eyes.

'Modest, isn't she?'

He trod on Arabella's long skirt, which was dragging on the ground.

Arabella spun round.

'This skirt is school property,' she said, glaring at him. 'I'll get in trouble if I damage it.'

In my opinion we had more important things to worry about than ripping Arabella's costume. Like trying to avoid being seen by a teacher for instance. And trying to stop our old arch-enemy from winning the Hornswaggle Boat Race. But that's the weird thing about Arabella. She minds more about damaging a school costume than she does about getting caught in a pirate battle. Arabella is not your average person.

In the school car park, she stopped so suddenly we all fell into each other. One of Bert's skimming stones fell out of the pillowcase and landed on my foot.

'Ow!' I shouted, giving Bert a thump.

'Ow back,' said Bert, flicking my nose.

'Quiet!' said Arabella, producing a large black key. She held it up. She looked very pleased with herself.

'What's so great about that?' asked Bert.

Arabella winked.

'Wait and see,' she said, pressing a small button on the key. Something beeped to our right and we spun round. It was a school bus.

'What do you think?' said Arabella. 'I stole (well, borrowed) the key from the store cupboard.'

'Blinking blowfish,' muttered Bert.

'Bum!' shrieked Maud.

'What on earth is going on here!' shouted a teacher, running towards us. Arabella opened the door of the school bus and grinned.

'Hurry up,' she said. 'Last one on is a blobfish!' Bert was the last on, and the door slammed behind him.

'Do you know how to drive it?' I asked.

'Oh yes,' said Arabella breezily. 'Dad lets me drive his new ride-on lawnmower whenever I like. Buses are just like lawnmowers.'

She sat in the driver's seat and turned on the

engine. The bus jumped in the air.

'Sorry about that,' said Arabella. 'Wrong gear!'

She tried again. The bus jumped even higher this time.

'Hang on a sec!' said Arabella. 'I forgot the clutch.'

'Baddie,' said Maud, pointing out of the window. 'Baddie!'

The teacher who had been shouting at us across the car park was now trying to force open the door of the bus. She looked very determined.

'Hurry!' I told Arabella.

Arabella pulled on the gear stick and the bus lurched backwards at top speed. The teacher fell over in surprise.

'I'm really sorry, Mrs Marshall,' shouted Arabella. 'I promise I didn't mean to make you fall over. I'm trying to go forwards not backwards!'

Mrs Marshall got to her feet and started to pick bits of car park out of her smart cardigan. She frowned at Arabella with a puzzled expression.

Arabella turned to me. 'Mrs Marshall is a REALLY

good maths teacher,' she said, fiddling with the gear stick. She suddenly looked anxious. 'Do you think she recognised me?'

'Stop worrying about your blinking maths teacher,' spluttered Bert. 'And get us out of here!'

Arabella slammed her foot down on the accelerator and the bus lurched forward at top speed. Bert, Maud and I fell flat on our backs. I was just about to tell Arabella that she was the worst driver in the world when I saw the car park gate whizz past the windows. When I pulled myself to my feet and looked back I spotted Mrs Marshall shaking her fist in the distance.

I rubbed a bruise on my arm and laughed. Arabella was driving the school bus like she'd been doing it her whole life. She grinned at me.

'Shabbers-on-Sea, here we come!'

CHAPTER
9

'What's the time?' I asked Arabella as we sped down the hill through the town.

'11.12 a.m. exactly,' she said, glancing at her watch.

'That means we only have forty-eight minutes until the race starts,' I said.

We passed a signpost that said Shabbers-on-Sea was fifteen miles away by road.

Arabella laughed.

'No problem,' she said. 'Sit back and enjoy the ride!'

I still didn't know how we were going to get our boat back from Captain Guillemot. And I still didn't dare to imagine what had happened to Mum and Dad. But we were on our way and, right now, that was all we could hope for.

'Bleughghghghghghhghghgh!'

Bert was sick all over the back seat.

'Do you have to do that?' said Arabella. 'It's rather distracting.'

Bert stuck out his tongue at Arabella's back but Arabella didn't notice.

'Goodness this is fun,' she said. 'I might ask Dad for driving lessons for my next birthday. I think I'm a natural.'

The bus lurched to one side. We had to hold on to the seats to stop ourselves from falling over. Well, all of us apart from George, who was sewing a small teddy bear.

'For your information,' spluttered Bert, 'it's not my fault I'm bus-sick. Pirates aren't used to roads.'

'*I'm* not sicky,' Maud told George. 'I'm not a sicky girl!'

Maud didn't even flinch when Arabella raced over a speed bump and the bus took to the air. She was too busy sticking out her tongue at the lorry driver behind us. George tried to distract her by handing her the finished teddy but she chucked it out of the window.

'Ooops!' said Maud, giggling at George and opening her huge brown eyes. George grinned.

'Can't you slow down a bit!' gasped Bert.

'Slow down?' said Arabella, scathingly. 'I thought you said the race starts in forty-eight minutes. I need to go faster, not slower.'

Arabella pulled the bus from side to side. Luckily Shabbers-on-Sea was well signposted. She turned left, then right, then left again. She got up to 80 m.p.h. on the dual carriageway. Finally, she jerked the bus onto a small, winding country lane.

'What glorious foliage!' she said, pointing out of the window. 'Red campion, valerian, rosebay willowherb, cowslips, dog roses, meadowsweet, foxgloves. You can't beat the English countryside in June can you? Hedgerows are nature's Persian rugs. That's what my dad always says.'

'We're pirates, we don't care about the blinking hedgerows, we don't care about purple rugs or whatever they're called,' Bert said, wiping his mouth. 'Just get us to Shabbers-on-Sea before I die.'

For once I'm not even sure Bert was exaggerating.

His skin had turned grey and he was all shiny. I was just beginning to wonder if maybe we needed to stop and get him to a doctor when Arabella put her foot on the brake and the bus skidded to a halt.

'Bob's your uncle,' she said, pointing down a hill.

'No he isn't,' spluttered Bert. 'Our uncle is called Roy and he's really really . . . Oh.'

Bert stopped and stared. Below us was a busy seaside town. We could see ramshackle buildings and plastic sheets flapping in the wind. We could hear seagulls shrieking. There were bright-coloured shops full of buckets and spades and postcards.

There were cafes selling chips and hot chocolate. There were scruffy donkeys giving rides along the harbour and there was an old merry-go-round with flaking paint.

Shabbers-on-Sea was grubby and tacky.

Shabbers-on-Sea was just our kind of place.

Bert was right, we pirates hate the countryside. Give us a rundown seaside town any day of the week. But unlike most rundown seaside towns, Shabbers-on-Sea wasn't deserted. It was heaving.

In the oily water of the harbour, loads of sailing boats jostled for space along a start line, turning circles impatiently like horses before a big race. Dotted around them were smaller motorboats carrying spectators and people with cameras. Back on shore, hundreds of people were rushing towards the harbour's old stone jetty.

'There you go,' said Arabella, pointing at the jetty. She sounded very pleased with herself. 'One family ship and one arch-enemy. You're welcome.'

CHAPTER 10

Seeing your own pirate ship makes you forget your troubles. Sometimes when Dad is feeling glum he likes to go ashore just so he can stand on the beach, gaze at *Sixpoint Sally* and cheer himself up. Mum says an eyeful of *Sally* is better than a skinful of rum.

For a few seconds after I spotted our pirate ship tied to that stone jetty, I stopped worrying about Mum and Dad and I stopped feeling nervous about the Hornswaggle Boat Race. I just felt really, really happy.

'She looks good,' Bert said.

To non-pirates, *Sixpoint Sally* probably looked like a slightly scruffy, rather old-fashioned sailing boat. But to us, she was the finest ship in the harbour. The problem was, it was obvious to me that *Sixpoint Sally* wasn't the *only* pirate ship in Shabbers-on-Sea. Over at the start line, gliding menacingly amongst the non-pirate boats, were three others – and they were Snazzy with a capital S.

I pointed at an enormous purple schooner.

'That's *Rum Punch*,' I muttered to Arabella and George. 'She has a gold ship's wheel and a platinum-plated mast.'

'Style over substance!' replied Arabella. 'It takes more than a bit of bling to frighten me.'

Bert spluttered furiously.

'A bit of bling?' he shouted. 'Have you even SEEN the crew?'

'Hmmmm,' said Arabella, narrowing her eyes at the pirates who were busy getting *Rum Punch* ready for sea. They had long curly hair and ratty ginger beards and they were huge. 'They are rather unpleasant-looking.'

I sighed. 'They're the Rattle-Dazzlers – A.K.A. the heftiest swashbucklers in Britain. And they're even more unpleasant than they look.'

Further along from *Rum Punch* was a turquoise ketch with the word *Swallow* written in navy-blue italics across her bow. She was the sleekest ship in the harbour. She was also full of pirates. This lot were smaller than the Rattle-Dazzlers and they were slim and wiry. They were up the mast and all over the rigging. A muscly woman in Lycra seemed to be in charge and doing a lot of shouting.

'That's Samantha Swigger,' said Bert. 'She does one hundred press-ups before breakfast.'

I nodded. 'The Swiggers are from Cornwall and their ship is the fastest in history.

We haven't seen them since the last race. They won it by a nautical mile.'

The third pirate ship was wedged between two fishing boats. It had peeling paint and a rusty anchor and it was called the *Spirit of Skegness*. Its deck was crowded with children. They were thin and pale with matted hair and dirty feet. They were having a water fight.

'The O'Drearys,' I explained to Arabella and George, 'and their nine children.'

'We used to have pirate play dates with 'em,' said Bert, peering at his old pal Dylan O'Dreary who had climbed to the top of the mast and was picking his nose and eating it. 'But we had to stop inviting them cos they kept stealing all our food. Their mum only lets them eat stuff you find in the sea – like fish and limpets and weed. They're permanently starving.'

'Absolutely charming!' said Arabella. 'I wish I had my paintbrush.'

Bert leaped to his feet.

'You don't paint pirate ships!' he spluttered, turning very red in the face. 'You attack them.'

'Well go on then,' said Arabella. 'Go and attack them if you're such a big brave boy.'

Bert kicked the side of the bus. I sighed. Although it was great to see *Sixpoint Sally*, we couldn't exactly start celebrating. There was also no sign of Mum and Dad – and finding them was just as important as getting back our ship and competing in the Hornswaggle Boat Race.

Arabella put on her glasses and peered at *Sixpoint Sally.*

'I don't believe it,' she said. 'That's a downward dog or I'm the Queen of England.'

Bert and I sniggered.

'Erm, I hate to burst your bubble,' I said. 'But I think you're seeing things. There's no dog there.'

Arabella laughed. 'A downward dog is a stretching posture, you wallies.'

She let the glasses fall to the end of her nose and looked down at us.

'Oh for heaven's sake,' she sighed. 'A downward dog is yoga.'

Bert and I still didn't have a clue what she was on about.

'Yoga,' said Arabella grandly, 'is a Hindu spiritual discipline, which includes breath control, simple mediation and the adoptions of bodily postures. It is used to aid health and relaxation.'

We stared at her blankly.

'They're stretching before the race,' she snapped. 'Guillemot must have learned yoga in that spa hotel of his.'

'In that case,' I said, trying to sound way more confident than I felt, 'we need to get down there right now and stop him.'

The fact that Guillemot and his crew had their bottoms in the air might just give us a chance. We hopped back on the bus and Arabella drove us down the hill to Shabbers-on-Sea.

The town centre was so full of spectators we had to park the bus on the high street and make our way to the harbour on foot. As we pushed our way through the crowds, Maud shouted insults from over George's shoulder.

"Ello, baldy!' she said to one man. "Ello, chickenpox!' she told a girl with freckles.

'You should make her apologise,' said Arabella, looking shocked.

'There's no point,' I said. 'She doesn't care about being rude. She doesn't care about being told off. She's never said sorry in her life.'

'She's the naughtiest toddler on the south coast,' said Bert, grinning.

Arabella sighed. 'She's getting worse.'

'I know,' I said proudly. 'She's a menace.'

When we reached the stone jetty, I signalled to the others to crouch down behind a pile of old lobster pots. Guillemot and the other pirates were now close enough to spit at and we couldn't risk being spotted – not until we had come up with a plan.

Right now the harbour looked busier than ever. As well as the four pirate ships there were about thirty non-pirate crews getting ready to race and they were all making last-minute preparations. The smaller boats carrying spectators and officials looked like they were nearly ready too.

'Look over there,' I said, pointing to a tall woman in a shiny speedboat. 'That's Dame Kittiwake.'

The woman wore a headscarf and pearls. She was holding a clipboard in one hand and an enormous megaphone in the other.

'Who is Dame Kittiwake when she's at sea?' demanded Arabella, narrowing her eyes and peering at the large scar on the woman's cheek.

'Dame Kittiwake,' I explained, 'is pirate royalty. She holds the record for the most Hornswaggle wins in history – and she did it all single-handed after the rest of the Kittiwakes emigrated to the Caribbean. When she retired from racing she became the chairwoman of the Royal Hornwswaggle Yacht Club. She organises this whole race. None of these non-pirates have a clue who she really is. They think she made her money running a boat-hire business.'

We all went quiet. Dame Kittiwake was not a woman we wanted to get on the wrong side of. Not only is she the person who starts the Hornswaggle Boat Race (hence the megaphone), she also follows the boats all the way out to Hornswaggle Rock and keeps an eye on anyone who tries to break the rules. At the end of the race, she presents the Treasurescope to the winner.

'She doesn't miss a trick,' said Bert gloomily. 'Remember the last race? She disqualified us for switching on our motor in Shipwreck Strait.'

'That's nothing,' I replied. 'Mum says she once sent the Rattle-Dazzlers back to Scotland for taking a shortcut.'

'Don't like her,' said Maud, sticking out her chin. 'She's a horridy.'

'Maud, shhh,' I warned. 'Dame Kittiwake is a VERY IMPORTANT PERSON.'

As if to prove my point, Dame Kittiwake chose that moment to pick up her megaphone.

'Sailors!' she boomed. 'You have twenty minutes until the start of the race. Final preparations please.'

There was a brief silence followed by a noisy mess of loud voices, flapping sails and creaking anchors. Hordes of spectators jostled for space along the stone quay like greedy seagulls. Dame Kittiwake watched the commotion through narrowed eyes and picked up her megaphone again.

'And can I remind competitors that you are *not* allowed to use an engine and you are *not* allowed to take any shortcuts. Apart from that you can cheat as much as you like!'

The crowd burst out laughing.

'They think she's joking,' I said, shaking my head. 'But it's true. As long as you sail the whole thing and don't take any shortcuts, cheating is allowed.'

Arabella frowned.

'What I don't understand is what all these non-pirates are doing here. Nobody around here approves of pirates.'

'They don't realise it's a pirate race,' I explained. 'They think the Hornswaggle is a posh sailing club that holds a famous sailing regatta once every four years. These crews actually think they have a chance of winning but of course they don't have a hope against us pirates.'

'Even if you do say so yourself!' said Arabella in her teacher voice. 'Well I suppose that explains the journalists.'

'The what?' frowned Bert.

'You know,' Arabella told him, 'the people who write newspapers and present the news on the TV and radio. The people over there with the cameras and microphones.'

We looked over to where Arabella was pointing.

Sure enough, over by the harbour master's hut, a little further on from where *Sixpoint Sally* was tied up, there was a group of men and women, chatting and laughing. Next to them was a large stack of cameras and microphones.

'I expect they're here to interview the different crews,' Arabella said.

'Captain Guillemot would LOVE that,' I said.

I paused.

'Wait here,' I said, chewing my lip. 'I have an idea.'

I dashed over to the reporters. In the middle of the group was a woman in a large padded red coat. Next to her was a camera and a microphone. She was talking to all the other journalists about a recent assignment.

'When I was in the Serengeti last October, a pack of lions turned and looked at me and I swear to you I thought my time was up.'

The other journalists nodded.

'When you're filming wild animals, you have to have your wits about you at all times,' she continued. 'Even when I'm not on a job, I'm on a permanent state of alert. I have to be. I never switch off. Even now I'm ready to react the moment I feel under attack.'

I stuck out my hand and picked up her camera and microphone. I waited for the famous journalist's high-alert reactions to kick in but she was too busy talking to notice me.

So I turned and legged it back to the others.

CHAPTER

11

'What are those for?' asked Arabella and Bert at the same time.

I handed George the camera.

Maud, who was still on his shoulders, began chewing the lens.

'My tooths!' she said when I tried to stop her.

'Teeth, for cretin's sake,' corrected Arabella. 'Teeth, not tooths.'

Maud laughed and carried on chewing.

'Excellent,' I told George. 'The camera completely covers your face.'

'What's so good about that?' asked Arabella.

I forgot that I hadn't yet told them my plan.

'Well,' I said. 'Guillemot is the vainest person we know, right?'

'Right,' said Bert and Arabella.

George just listened.

'So if he thinks there's a chance to get on telly, he's going to be keen. Right?'

'Yeeeeessss,' said Arabella, more slowly this time.

'So if we pretend to be TV journalists, we'll have a chance of getting on board our ship. And if George's face is hidden by the camera, Guillemot won't know it's him.'

Arabella stood up and sucked in her cheeks. 'Don't even think about sending my brother off by himself to do your dirty work.' She tried to pull the camera out of George's hands.

'Wait,' I whispered. 'It has to be George because he's big enough to look like a grown-up. But don't worry,' I said. 'He won't be alone.'

I paused and handed the microphone to Arabella.

'He's going to have you with him.'

Arabella laughed scornfully.

'This is SO typical,' she said. 'You so-called toughies are sending your poor defenceless non-pirate pals on board to fight your old arch-enemy because you're too cowardly to do it yourselves. Some pirates *you* are.'

'It's not like that,' I said. 'We can't go ourselves. If Guillemot so much as catches sight of a McScurvy he'll tie us up and turn us into fish food before we can say "Ouch". But if this goes to plan, Captain Guillemot won't suspect a thing. You're in costume, remember. Which means there's a good chance Guillemot won't recognise you. After all, *we* didn't and we're your best friends.'

Arabella nodded.

'You can pretend to be a reporter and George can be your cameraman. All you have to do is distract Guillemot into thinking he's going to be on telly, then we can all hop aboard and take over the ship.' I paused. 'You *are* a great actor.'

Arabella started to smirk.

'Well,' she sighed. 'I'm just passionate about my

craft, that's all. I just love to immerse myself in a role. But there's one problem. How do we get them off the boat?'

I hadn't thought of this.

'Could you push them overboard?' I suggested half-heartedly.

'Too risky,' Arabella said, frowning. 'On the other hand, you've just given me an idea . . . '

I left Arabella mid-thought and glanced over at *Sixpoint Sally*. The yoga session seemed to have finished. Captain Guillemot was now untying ropes and shouting orders. Cath was pulling fenders over the side of rigging. Bones was studying a tatty map. Beefster was hauling sails. They were still wearing their fluffy white bathrobes but this didn't stop them looking very VERY bloodthirsty.

Arabella put on her glasses and hat and stood up. She tidied her hair. She blew some dust off the microphone.

'Come on, George,' she said, putting on her best acting voice. 'Take off your school tie and jumper, undo your collar and get into character.

Imagine you're a famous cameraman. Immerse yourself in the world of investigative journalism.'

Arabella swirled her skirt and flicked her hair. She closed her eyes. George picked up the camera, plonked it on his shoulder and followed Arabella over to *Sixpoint Sally*.

We crept after them, hiding ourselves among the feet of the crowd, taking care not to be seen.

'George,' sobbed Maud. 'I want George.'

Luckily Maud's cries were drowned out by the sound of a foghorn and Dame Kittiwake's voice booming down the microphone again.

'You have just ten minutes left, sailors. Will all the crews prepare their vessels for the start of the race? We want bows pointed towards the sea and sterns touching the harbour wall. Good luck!'

My heart sank. Ten minutes wasn't long enough to get Guillemot off our boat. Any minute now he would cast off the ropes and start sailing *Sixpoint Sally* towards the start line.

'Bum,' said Maud. 'Bum bum bum.'

I shut my eyes.

'Yes, Maud,' I said. 'For once I agree with you. This situation is a complete and utter . . . '

'My name is Hattie Headline,' said a woman's voice. 'I work for the BBC and I was just wondering if we could get some pre-race footage of you and your crew.'

I blinked. Arabella and George were standing on the bridge of our pirate ship. Arabella turned round and gave me the very faintest wink. Then she turned back to face Captain Guillemot.

'With your classic bone structure,' she continued, 'I have a feeling that you are a very photogenic young man. How do you feel about being the FACE OF THE RACE?'

Captain Guillemot sucked in his cheeks and smiled. I let out a deep sigh of relief. He definitely hadn't recognised Arabella.

'Hmm,' he said, smirking. 'I bet that's what you say to all the sailors.'

'Good heavens no!' said Arabella. 'Most sailors are shabby old soaks. We've been looking for someone REALLY handsome and photogenic – and HERE YOU ARE!'

'I see what you're saying,' said Guillemot, smiling broadly and puffing out his chest. 'I suppose I do have a face for telly – always have done, always will – but I'm a bit busy getting things shipshape right now. Can't you interview me after the race? When I've won the Treasurescope?'

Arabella smiled.

'Oh dear,' she said. 'My editor specifically wants some pre-race footage. But don't worry, if you haven't got time, I'll go and ask the Swiggers.'

Arabella and George turned to leave.

'Wait!' Guillemot said. 'It's fine. I can spare a minute or two. If you need a FACE OF THE RACE, I'm your man.'

'Excellent!'

Arabella beckoned to George. She looked around wildly. I could tell by the way she was smiling secretly to herself that she was plotting something.

'We'd like to film you standing on your gang plank with the sea behind you? Is that OK?'

'Fine, fine,' said Guillemot, trying out different poses and gathering his crew around him. 'Whatever you think is best Miss . . .'

'Headline,' purred Arabella. 'Hattie Headline.'

Guillemot and his crew flung off their towelling bathrobes. Underneath they were wearing matching red shorts.

'You may as well see the real me,' Guillemot told Arabella, grinning nastily. 'Six-pack and all.'

Arabella backed away from Guillemot's toothy gold smile.

'Great idea,' she said. 'You just stand there on the plank and we'll start to film. I don't need to tell you to look handsome.' She giggled. 'Just try to look natural.'

Guillemot and his crew stood obediently in line. I wondered again if Mum and Dad were still asleep below deck or if Guillemot had chucked them overboard. If he had, then right now they would be swimming for their lives, hoping to be rescued. Just thinking about this made me shiver.

'Ask me anything you like,' said Guillemot. 'Ask me how it feels to be the FACE OF THE RACE. Ask me where I bought my red trunks. Ask me how rich I am. Ask me how I manage to keep my skin so smooth. Ask me where I get my hair done.'

'Oh I will, I will,' said Arabella. 'But I still need you to move back a bit. My cameraman can't get you all in shot.'

Guillemot moved a step back and gestured to Beefster, Bones and Cath to do the same.

'Better?'

Arabella turned to George.

'Hmmmm, it's still a bit tricky to get you all in,' she said, thoughtfully. 'Isn't it, Fergus?'

George nodded from behind the camera.

'One more step back should do it,' smiled Arabella.

Guillemot and his crew took another tiny step back.

'Excellent,' squeaked Arabella. I could hear the excitement in her voice. 'Wonderful expressions. I was right, you are SOOOOOO photogenic. It's all about bone structure, you see – and your hair is such a wonderful colour. I'd love to get the name of your stylist. But if you could move back just a teensy bit more, I think we'll get a really brilliant shot. Is that possible?'

'Sure,' said Guillemot. 'I'm the FACE OF THE RACE, I'm not camera-shy.'

Guillemot and his crew took another step back. But this time there was no plank left for them to step on.

They all fell backwards into the water.

'My hair!' bellowed Guillemot, desperately trying to keep his head above water. 'I've just had it coloured, I'm not supposed to get it wet!'

Arabella whipped off her glasses and hat and showed her real face and hair to Captain Guillemot.

He recognised her at once. 'Ginger nut?!!!!' he roared.

Arabella burst out laughing.

'Ahoy there,' she said. 'I'm afraid you're not going to work as our FACE OF THE RACE after all.' She giggled. 'You're a bit too . . . old.'

Guillemot roared.

'I'm not OLD!' he spluttered.

George ran to put the camera down on the jetty and helped Bert, Maud and me to leap on board.

'This lot are much younger,' Arabella shouted at Guillemot and his crew. 'And they're way more piratey too.'

Guillemot spat out a mouthful of water and started to swim back to the boat.

'Robbers!' he shouted up at us. 'Thieves! Cheats!'

'Takes one to know one,' I laughed.

BOOOOOM!

The sound of a foghorn echoed around the harbour again. The large crowd began to shout and cheer in excitement. There was a deafening flapping sound as thirty assorted sailing ships hoisted their mainsails and tightened their spinnakers.

'**On your marks!**' boomed Dame Kittwake down the megaphone.

Bert grabbed the rope of the mainsail.

'**Get set!**'

I pulled on the ship's wheel.

'**Go!**'

The crowd jumped up and down as the colourful mix of sailing boats headed out to sea.

The Hornswaggle Boat Race had begun.

CHAPTER
12

'Please let Mum and Dad be down here,' I whispered to myself as I stepped into *Sixpoint Sally*'s cabin. 'Please.'

But of course their bunks were empty. Which meant only one thing. Guillemot must have chucked them overboard. Probably somewhere back in the Bay of Barnacles.

I sighed, opened a hidden locker above the stove and pulled out a pink velvet box.

Inside was the Blighty Bling, glittering as if it were winking at me.

'What should I do?' I whispered to the famous jewel. 'Go in search of Mum and Dad? Or try to win this race?'

The Blighty Bling winked away. It didn't give me any answers. I sighed and put it round my neck.

Deep down I knew that Mum wouldn't want us to give up now – not after all the training she'd put us through. We had to keep going, however hopeless things seemed. I returned to the deck.

'Any sign of them?' asked Bert.

I shook my head.

Bert kicked the side of the ship.

'Can't we make her go any faster?' Arabella shouted.

I felt *Sally* creak as Bert pushed her into the wind.

'Can't YOU stop bossing us around?'

But Bert and I weren't really cross with Arabella. She had been brilliant. She had managed to trick four fully grown pirates into walking the plank. Plus she wasn't even boasting about it. If Bert or I had pulled off something like that, we would have bragged about it for at least ten years.

I took over from Bert at the wheel. The wind was getting stronger by the minute. Mum would have told us we had perfect sailing conditions but then Mum's muscles are about ten times the size of ours. She can keep Sally steady in a force-ten gale. She was born to race.

We, on the other hand, were born to eat sweets and muck around. We might be pirates but we're still just kids.

We were racing alongside a cluster of non-pirate sailing boats. The three pirate ships were already half a mile ahead. Dame Kittiwake was scudding alongside them in her top-of-the-range speedboat.

'Bum!' shouted Maud, bouncing on the pile of towelling bathrobes that Guillemot and his crew had left on board. She pulled a face at a boat full of journalists as we tried to overtake them. 'See you later, shark pants!' she cackled.

'*Sally* won't go any faster,' I told Arabella.

I knew that the Blighty Bling would show us the quickest way to Hornswaggle Rock, avoiding rocks and whirlpools. But I also knew that not even the Blighty Bling could make us go any faster. Nothing could do that.

'Well at least we don't have Guillemot to worry about any more,' Arabella said cheerfully. 'Look,' she said, pointing our telescope back towards Shabbers-on-Sea. 'He's having his moment of glory after all.'

I grabbed the telescope and looked towards the harbour. Arabella was right. Guillemot had now managed to climb out of the sea. His red swimming trunks were dripping with water and he was making sure his hair hadn't got wet. He was surrounded by another group of journalists.

'He's probably telling them some sob story about his boat being stolen,' said Arabella. '*His* boat indeed.'

'No one cares about the truth,' said Bert. 'You can cheat as much as you like in the Hornswaggle. Cheating's in the rules.'

'It makes no difference,' I said. 'Not even cheating can make us sail faster.'

'What if we chuck all the heavy stuff overboard – that'll speed things up,' suggested Bert.

Maud was chewing on a golden goblet. She looked at it and grinned.

'This is heavy!' she shouted. 'This is very really heavy.'

Maud hurled the golden goblet overboard and clapped when it made a big splash in the sea.

Then she reached into the nearest treasure chest for something else to throw.

I rushed forward.

'NO, Maud!' I shouted, closing the lid of the treasure chest. 'We can't start chucking away treasure, even if it does lighten our load. No pirate ever chucks away treasure.'

Maud ignored me and picked up a valuable gold watch. She got ready to throw.

'Maud!' I said in my strictest voice. 'If you chuck

away any more treasure, I will chuck away your nuggy.'

Maud stuck out her tongue.

'Meanie,' she shouted.

She started to scream. Maud's scream is the worst – and loudest – sound in the world. But, for once, George didn't come running. George had disappeared.

CHAPTER

13

I was just beginning to worry that George had fallen overboard when I heard Arabella shout.

'Over here!' She lifted up the pile of bathrobes. 'Oh,' she said proudly. 'Bravo, George!'

'Bravo?' spluttered Bert. 'Bravo? We're supposed to be winning a boat race, not hiding away practising embroidery.'

I looked over at George. Bert was right. George was sewing.

'You have got to be joking,' I said, turning back towards the sea. 'Pirates don't sew.'

'I never joke about my brother,' said Arabella.

'Well *I* do,' I said, not daring to take my eyes off the pirate ships ahead. 'I joke about my brother ALL the time. But, you know what, at least *my* brother can help sail a boat. At least *my* brother is capable of doing the odd dastardly deed. At least *my* brother is a teeny bit cutthroat, for shrimp's sake.'

I looked over at Bert. He was sucking on a lollipop. He did not look dastardly *or* cutthroat.

'Thanks, sis,' he said sticking a thumb up at me.

Arabella rolled her eyes.

'Oh for heaven's sake,' she sighed. 'I thought you wanted to *win* this race. I thought you wanted to catch up with those rival pirate crews. I thought you wanted to get your hands on that Treasurescope.'

'We do!' I said in my loudest voice. 'So maybe you can persuade your brother to start concentrating on SAILING rather than SEWING.'

Arabella went all huffy.

'Actually,' she began. 'George is—'

'Ignore them!' I said, turning to Bert. 'They're not pirates and never will be.'

'Honestly!' said Arabella. 'If you'd let me get a word in edge—'

'Tighten the jib,' I told Bert. 'We need to sail closer to the wind.'

Sally's sides creaked with the effort but it was no good. We just couldn't make her go any faster. The Swiggers were now a speck in the distance. The O'Drearys were close behind them, followed by the Rattle-Dazzlers.

Even worse, we were now being overtaken by one of the non-pirate boats. It was a large white catamaran with 'Corporate Sailing Experiences' written on its side. It was carrying a smartly dressed crew in matching yellow coats and bright red lifejackets. None of them looked as if they had ever even been on a boat before, let alone competed in a famous pirate race. They waved cheerfully as they swooshed past.

'They'll never beat us,' scowled Bert. 'They're just a bunch of office workers on a day out. We're the real pirates.'

But right now I wasn't sure that made any difference.

We had already lost our parents and our pet parrot. With the sort of luck we were having, I wouldn't have been surprised if we'd lost the race to a bunch of amateurs in a rented catamaran.

'Blimey,' said Bert.

'Bum!' shouted Maud.

'What now?' I snapped, turning around.

George grinned sheepishly.

'Here you go,' he said, handing me a neatly folded pile of white fluffy towels.

'Thanks, George,' I said. 'But we don't have time for a bath right now.'

Arabella started to laugh.

'It's not what you think it is, you numpty,' she said. 'Unfurl it, have a closer look . . .'

I sighed and started to unfold the pile of fluffy white material that had been plonked in my hands.

'Shiver me timbers,' I gasped. 'I see what you mean.'

CHAPTER

14

Pirates aren't good at EVERYTHING. Even Bert knows that. For example we're rubbish at knowing how to work an iPhone. We don't know who won World War Two. We haven't got the first clue how to *spell* trigonometry – let alone understand it. But we do understand other things. Thinks like . . . wind. We listen to the shipping forecast on Dad's homemade radio twice a day, we study the clouds and the sun. We sense changes in the air. Dad says all pirates have good windstinct. It's essential.

George may not be the cleverest boy at his

school but when I saw what he had been sewing I realised that George also has VERY good windstinct – and when you're a pirate, well, that's all that matters. George had used his sewing skills to turn the pile of white fluffy bathrobes into a brand-new sail. It was exactly what we needed.

'Come on,' said Arabella. 'Let's get this thing hoisted.'

That was easier said than done.

First we had to loop long ropes into the corners of George's sail, then we needed to tie it to the rigging. I made small holes in the sail with my cutlass, Arabella attached the ropes and Bert climbed up the rigging to tie it all to the mast. This was a dangerous job because *Sally* lurched and rolled each time she went over a wave.

'Don't let go,' I called out to Bert.

'Don't boss me around!' he replied.

'Go, Bert bum,' chanted Maud.

Sixpoint Sally lurched to the right. For the next
few minutes I concentrated on holding the Blighty
Bling up in the air and steering *Sally*. I didn't look up.
The truth is I was genuinely worried that Bert might
fall. My little brother might be a big fat pain but I
didn't want him to die.

A gust of wind blew across us and I felt *Sally* surge through the water. But this time she felt different. I looked at the foamy sea flashing past us in a blur of white spray and realised we were travelling at twice our previous speed.

I felt a huge smile spread across my face. George's bathrobe sail was working.

'Glorious!' said Arabella, as we overtook a motorboat full of spectators. 'Absolutely glorious.'

'We're not on holiday you know,' said Bert. 'We're not on a stupid school trip. We're in a famous pirate race and we're still coming last.'

'You pirates,' said Arabella, shaking her head. 'You're always so negative. Can't you look on the bright side for once? We've doubled our speed, we're leaving most of the non-pirates for flotsam, we're catching up with the others, we're in with a chance.'

She was right of course. Behind us, Shabbers-on-Sea was so far away it looked like a toy town. Apart from the annoying white catamaran that was just in front of us, most of the non-pirate sailing boats were now behind us. Even better, we were closing in on the colourful hulls of *Rum Punch*, *Swallow* and the *Spirit of Skegness*.

The problem was, I didn't have a clue what we were going to do when we DID catch up with them.

Mum had planned everything – from outwitting our rival pirates to plucking the flag from Hornswaggle Rock. We'd been so busy mucking around we hadn't listened properly.

'We may have come far,' I told Arabella, grabbing a handful of chocolate fingers from my pocket and shoving them all in my mouth at once. 'But we've still got a long way to go. There's no time to celebrate.'

I held up the Blighty Bling and steered *Sally* gently to the right. She glided through the waves, sending mouthfuls of salty water on to deck. I could hear the wind gathering behind her sails, pushing her faster and faster. I leaned forward.

'Come on, *Sally*,' I whispered. 'You can do it.'

You may not believe in magic but that's probably because you're not a pirate. When you spend your lives at sea with nothing but the wind and the sun for company you have more time for things like magic. And right now, I'm telling you – magic was in the air. The wind was casting invisible spells behind *Sally*'s sails. The sun was lighting a path through the waves. It was as if the sea gods had blessed *Sally* with their special powers.

Five minutes later we had overtaken the white catamaran and were alongside a boat full of journalists. It only took us another few minutes to catch up with *Rum Punch*.

'Ahoy there!' we waved at the Rattle-Dazzlers.

The Rattle-Dazzlers did not wave back.

They shouted and roared and said quite a few rude words – too rude to put in a children's book so I'm not allowed to repeat them here. But just so you know, they were so rude that Arabella's ears turned bright pink. For the next half mile we raced with them neck and neck.

Maud called Captain Rattle-Dazzler a Hairy Mary. We all laughed. I thought, Maybe everything is going to be OK. Maybe Mum and Dad have managed to reach the shore. Maybe it's all going to be fine.

Then . . .

. . . BUMP!

Sally lurched on to her side.

'Did we just hit a rock?' Arabella gasped.

George picked up Maud just before she rolled overboard. I looked down at the sea.

'No,' I whispered, my mouth turning drier than a washed-up whale bone. 'It's not a rock.'

CHAPTER 15

According to Granny McScurvy there are so many sharks in the water around Hornswaggle Rock that you can't avoid them, even if you have the Blighty Bling. She says your only hope is to scare them away before they eat you. Granny McScurvy says if she had a gold coin for every pirate who's been eaten by a shark in these waters, she'd be the richest woman in England. Granny McScurvy once lost her left thumb to a great white.

'It's a shark!' I gulped.

'And it's trying to bite our ship,' replied Arabella,

143

leaning over the side.

'That's what sharks do.' I sighed gloomily. 'They bite holes in the side of the boat until the boat fills with water. Then, when the boat sinks, they gobble the crew.'

Maud leaned over the side.

'I'll bite those meanies back!' she shouted as ten more sharks arrived.

But sharks aren't scared of pirates – not even bitey three-year-old menaces. Their teeth are sharper than a sword and cutlass rolled into one. Of course, great whites aren't normally found off the south coast of Britain but Dame Kittiwake always ships them in specially for the Hornswaggle Boat Race. She lures them here with the promise of gourmet lobster suppers and a day at a water park.

I heard a scraping sound coming from *Sally*'s hull and saw the white catamaran swerve to avoid sailing into the back of us. Everything went into slow motion. Over to our right, a speedboat of officials was keeping its distance. The group of sailing boats behind us began to panic and turn back to shore.

Dame Kittiwake's telescope glimmered in the sun as she kept an eye on the action. Camera flashes exploded like silent fireworks from the television crew's boat. Great, I thought, not only are we going to be eaten alive but we're going to be filmed as it happens.

I closed my eyes.

Swiiiiishhhhh!

Something small and round whizzed past my left ear and landed in the water below.

Swiiiiiishhhhh!

Something whistled past my right ear. I spun round. Bert's legs were bent and he was squinting down into the water. He pulled a stone out of his pillowcase and sent it whizzing through the air into the water.

The stone bounced off a shark's head, skimmed across the sea, and landed on several more sharks before it sank.

'Bingo!' shouted Bert, pulling out another stone and skimming it at the biggest shark.

There are some moments when I don't hate my little brother. This was one of those moments.

'But,' I said, 'those skimming stones are your pride and joy!'

Bert grinned. 'I know,' he said. 'And haven't I been telling you all these years . . . they are very, very useful.'

For the next few minutes, we stood on deck, working our way through Bert's collection of skimming stones and pounding the circling sharks.

'It's working!' said Bert. 'They're swimming away!'

'Even better than that,' said Arabella, laughing, 'They've jumped ship.'

CHAPTER
16

There is nothing more sinister than the sound of a boat splintering apart.

We watched as the sharks swam over to *Rum Punch* and started taking huge mouthfuls out of her hull. Captain Rattle-Dazzler's face turned the colour of raw salmon.

'You useless bunch of sick buckets!' he raged as his crew failed to poke the sharks away with anchor hooks.

Water began to slosh on board.

'All aboard the *Dodger*!' yelled Captain Rattle-

Dazzler, heading for a speedboat tied to the stern.

'He's making a getaway,' said Arabella.

'He can't be. Pirates don't abandon ships, especially not in the middle of the Hornswaggle Boat Race.'

'These ones do.'

Arabella was right. The five Rattle-Dazzlers piled into their speedboat. Then Captain Rattle-Dazzler switched on the engine and a loud whirring noise echoed around the sea as he sped away.

'Looks like they got out just in time,' said Arabella, pointing as *Rum Punch* lurched sideways and started to sink.

'This is worse than when Trigger died,' said Bert gloomily.

'Who's Trigger?' asked Arabella.

'Our pet crab,' explained Bert. 'He died from eating too many chocolate buttons. We buried him in a favourite corner of our favourite beach. We used a matchbox for a coffin and filled it with cheese crisps – cheese crisps were Trigger's second-favourite snack. Dad cried for weeks.'

Arabella snorted. But I knew what Bert meant. Seeing *Rum Punch* go down *was* almost like watching something die. *Rum Punch* was a living, breathing pirate ship. *Rum Punch* had taken years to build. *Rum Punch* was in the prime of her life. *Rum Punch* was the Rattle-Dazzlers' home. No pirate likes to see a sinking ship, even if it does belong to a rival family.

To make things worse, the television crews were filming it.

Arabella sighed.

'Just think of the stunning craftsmanship – all gone to waste at the bottom of the sea.'

I sighed too.

'Just think of the treasure.'

Maud chuckled.

'Just fink – the Rattle-Dazzlers are out of the race!'

I turned to the others.

'Maud's right. The Rattle-Dazzlers can't win the Hornswaggle, not now they're in a speedboat. You have to sail to win the Hornswaggle, remember. The musclemen are out of the way.'

Arabella grinned at me.

'One pirate ship down,' she said, pointing into the distance. 'Two to go.'

Swallow and the *Spirit of Skegness* disappeared between two small barren islands that stuck out like bulging eyes in the middle of the wide-open sea.

I didn't dare tell Arabella that, deep down, I felt our chances of overtaking those two pirate crews were less than zero.

'They've turned into Shipwreck Strait,' I said, gulping. 'I remember it from last time we entered. Shipwreck Strait leads you straight to Hornswaggle Rock. It's the toughest part of the race.'

CHAPTER
17

We sailed towards Shipwreck Strait in silence, sucking sweets and chewing gum. I hated the thought of having to navigate this dangerous stretch of water without Mum and Dad. For the hundredth time I wondered if we'd done the right thing competing in the race rather than trying to rescue them.

I turned to Bert.

'What do *you* think's happened to them?' I muttered.

'Who, the Rattle-Dazzlers?'

'No, you moron. Mum and Dad.'

'Oh,' said Bert and his voice cracked up. 'I suppose Guillemot must have chucked them overboard. But they're strong swimmers. They'll be OK. Won't they?'

I looked down at some water that was sloshing over my feet.

Maybe we should go and find them,' I said. 'Maybe we should have done that in the first place.'

'But we're in the middle of the race!' said Bert. 'We can't quit NOW.'

Sixpoint Sally cut determinedly through the water like a cutlass through a flag. She didn't want to turn back any more than Bert did.

'All right!' I snapped. 'We'll keep going.' I told myself that the closer Mum and Dad swam to shore, the more chance they'd have of being picked up by someone. But the blood running through my veins was icy cold. I knew I'd never forgive myself if they drowned.

I glanced back and was relieved to see that most of the non-pirate boats had retired and the white catamaran was now trailing in our wake. I blocked out the shouts and calls of the spectators and journalists who were following close behind us. I steered *Sixpoint Sally* carefully between the two islands.

Shipwreck Strait turned out to be more like a surging river than the sea. It felt like a completely new ocean with a different weather system. The water that sprayed our faces was cold, the air was dark, and the clouds seemed to descend from the sky like huge spiders on invisible cobwebs.

But our real problem was the current. Shipwreck Strait was a mass of tides and whirlpools that kept changing direction. I remember Mum telling us that it has something to do with the two islands being so close. The land creates its own tidal system that then pushes against the main tide, creating a surge.

At times we were pulled along so fast that we barely needed sails. Then we'd be snapped back and snatched away again. *Sixpoint Sally* bumped and swayed and spun. On deck we were flung to the side and knocked to the ground. The boom kept swinging across the ship and if we didn't duck in time we would have been knocked overboard.

Dame Kittiwake sped up and down the strait in her smart speedboat, checking that no one was switching on a hidden engine. But we didn't need to use our engine. Thanks to George's homemade sail we were sailing along quite strongly. We even began to catch up with the O'Drearys.

Soon we were close enough to hear Mrs O'Dreary yelling at her children.

'Tighten the spinnaker!' she shouted. 'I don't want to have to ask you again.'

The O'Dreary children ran wildly across the

decks and ignored their mum. Dylan O'Dreary
turned to me and fired a catapult at my head.
I ducked.

'You'll never beat us without your parents,' he
yelled. 'There's eleven of us and only five of you.
Plus we've got catapults. You're well and truly
outnumbered and you're . . .'

He paused.

'. . . you're eating sour-grape lollies,' he
whispered.

Bert pulled his lolly out of his mouth.

'Actually,' he slurped. 'It's cherry cola.'

Dylan O'Dreary swallowed. A bit of dribble ran down his chin.

A small girl with matted hair and huge sludgy green eyes turned to stare at us.

'We're not allowed cherry cola,' she said, putting down her catapult. 'We're not allowed lollies.'

'Cherry cola?' shrieked a skinny toddler in a filthy nappy. 'Where's the cherry cola?'

'Bit peckish are you?' I laughed, opening a packet of crisps and eating them as slowly as I could, savouring every mouthful.

'Told you their parents won't let them eat junk food,' I muttered to Arabella and George. 'That's why they're so keen on trying to get their hands on ours.'

Delia O'Dreary, who was halfway up the mast, spun her bony head in my direction.

'Is someone,' she whispered, twitching her nose, 'eating salt and vinegar chipsticks?'

I laughed and crunched loudly.

Arabella turned to me.

'How much food do you guys have left?' she asked.

'Loads,' I said. 'We filled our pockets and everything. We've got enough to keep us going for the whole race.'

Arabella nodded.

'Thought so,' she said, winking and looking just like a real pirate. 'Then let's use it as bait to get the O'Drearys off their boat and out of the race.'

'That,' I said, throwing my salt and vinegar chipsticks into the sea, 'is an excellent plan.'

Delia O'Dreary dived in to grab the crisps.

'That was easy!' said Arabella, hooting with laughter. 'Let's see what else tickles their taste buds.'

I grinned and threw in some chocolate fingers. Arabella lobbed in a pack of Hula Hoops. George laid a trail of iced buns. Even Maud gave away a jar of strawberry sherbets.

'Help yourselves!' shouted Bert as he flung his entire stash of chocolate buttons into the sea.

Our plan worked brilliantly. The O'Dreary kids were so desperate for decent food that soon all nine of them were in the sea, fighting each other for sweets and shovelling goodies into their mouths.

'Get back on board!' shouted their mum. 'You're not allowed unrefined sugar. Get that filthy muck out of your mouths.'

But the nine O'Dreary children ignored her. They hadn't tasted food this good for months and nothing was going to stop them from scoffing it.

'Look!' I said, as the children drifted away from their ship. 'They're being washed down Shipwreck Strait.'

'Come back at once,' shouted Mrs O'Dreary. 'I've got some homemade smoked-mackerel pâté on board.'

But even if the children had wanted homemade smoked-mackerel pâté (which I doubted) they would never have been able to swim back to their boat. The current was far too strong.

Mrs O'Dreary shouted desperately at her husband.

'We have to turn back.'

'Really?' said Mr O'Dreary, frowning. 'They're good swimmers aren't they, someone will pick them up. After all we've got a race to win.'

'We've got nine children,' shrieked Mrs O'Dreary hysterically, 'and they're being whisked away in front of our eyes! If we don't go and rescue them, they'll drift out to the shark pool.'

Mr O'Dreary scowled.

'It's about time,' he said, furiously switching on the engine and turning the *Spirit of Skegness* around, 'that our children learned to listen.'

'I know,' sighed Mrs O'Dreary. 'I'll tell them they can't go swimming for a month.'

Dame Kittiwake picked up her megaphone.

'Illegal engine use!' she bellowed. 'O'Drearys, you are DISQUALIFIED!'

Our cheers were so loud they drowned out Mrs O'Dreary's shrieks.

CHAPTER
18

The air got colder the further we sailed up Shipwreck Strait. The islands either side of us were covered in marram grass and purple heather. They were edged by steep rocky cliffs crowded with seagulls and puffins. I couldn't see one single tree.

Arabella shuddered.

'I wouldn't want to live out here,' she said. 'What would you do if you fancied seeing the latest film at the cinema? Where would you go for brunch?'

I rolled my eyes.

'That's the thing about islands – they're deserted. That's why we pirates love them so much. No metal detectors, no police. We can hide our treasure in safety.'

Arabella sniggered.

'Yes, that's what I've always admired about you lot, the way you look after your treasure. I mean you never lose anything precious do you – not the Blighty Bling, not your pirate ship, NOT YOUR PARENTS.'

'Actually,' I snapped, 'we didn't LOSE our parents. They were kidnapped.'

I was about to start telling her that I knew Mum and Dad were absolutely fine, that they would have swum to safety by now. But I stopped. I wasn't sure myself.

'Our mum and dad are the best pirates in the world,' shouted Bert crossly. 'No need to worry about them.'

Arabella shook her head. I took a gulp of air and swallowed as the cool saltiness rushed through my body. Behind us, still battling their way through the current were four boats – the white catamaran, two large motorboats full of spectators and a smaller one carrying the television crew.

Alongside us was Dame Kittiwake. She was clutching her clipboard and megaphone. She had her eyes fixed on the Swiggers ahead of us.

'So,' said Arabella. 'What's the McScurvy race plan? How are we going to beat the Swiggers this close to the finish?'

'Well . . .' I told her, 'I don't know.'

'I thought you said your mum's been training you for weeks.'

'She has,' I said. 'The problem is, I can't remember what she said. I wasn't listening.' I felt my face turn bright red.

'Are you telling me,' said Arabella, 'that we've stolen a school bus, dressed up as journalists, constructed a new sail, saved ourselves from a giant shoal of killer sharks, seen off two pirate crews and sailed most of the way down Shipwreck Strait only to fall at the last hurdle?'

I shrugged.

'The Swiggers are quite a last hurdle,' I said, pointing as *Swallow* sailed out of Shipwreck Strait.

'There it is!' shouted Bert. 'There's Hornswaggle Rock.'

Even from a mile away there was no mistaking the famous rock. It was huge and black and it was shaped like a rhino horn. On its tip flapped a chequered flag embroidered with a golden Treasurescope.

'What a fascinating example of sea erosion!' said Arabella. 'If only I had my camera, I could take a picture of it for Mrs Manners, my geography teacher. We studied unusual rock formations last term.'

'Fascinating?' gulped Bert, glaring at Arabella. '*Fascinating?* Hornswaggle Rock is more than a geographical landmark, it's-it's-it's . . .!'

'It's a place where dreams are made or broken,' I said. I'd never felt this determined. 'So let's stop the Swiggers getting there first!'

Sometimes you don't need a plan. Sometimes you just need to go as fast as you can.

We pushed *Sally* into the wind as we passed through the remaining bit of Shipwreck Strait and out into open sea.

In the boats behind us, spectators were beginning to cheer. I heard television directors ordering their crews to get ready to film the finish. Dame Kittiwake boomed into a walkie-talkie.

'Yes,' she said. 'It's looking like a Swiggers' victory again.'

I groaned loudly.

'Oh honestly,' said Arabella. 'Where's your pirate spirit? Where's your gumption? Where's your— Yikes!'

We all jumped as a dishevelled parrot landed on our ship's wheel.

'Pedro!' I said crossly. 'Where have you been? You're meant to be helping us. Mum and Dad need rescuing.'

Pedro flapped his feathers. He looked grumpier than ever. I scribbled a note on a bit of old sail and tied it round his leg.

'Pedro,' I said. 'Mum and Dad are stuck in the Bay of Barnacles without a boat. You need to fly to Granny McScurvy and give her this note.'

I began to feel hopeful that we might just be able to rescue Mum and Dad after all. You don't have to be a pirate to know that birds fly faster than helicopters and cars – and definitely faster than any old boat. If Pedro started flying right now, he'd be at Granny McScurvy's houseboat in less than ten minutes.

But Pedro didn't start flying. Pedro ignored me. He was gazing at a speeding flash of pink and green feathers. I groaned again.

'What now?' asked Arabella. 'That bird that just flew past,' I explained, 'is called Pamela, and Pedro's in love with her. When she's around, Pedro doesn't listen to a word we say.'

Pamela was heading for the top of *Swallow*'s crow's nest.

'Oh dear,' said Arabella, looking through her telescope. 'I think Pedro may have some competition.'

She pointed. Sitting up in *Swallow*'s crow's nest, preening his feathery crest, was a large, handsome scarlet macaw. Pedro took one look at his new love rival and flew full pelt towards *Swallow*.

'Pedro!' I called. 'Watch out!'

PLIP!

Pedro flew beak-first into the Swiggers' mainsail. There was a loud hissing sound. For a few seconds, Pedro was stuck. He flapped his wings and wriggled his body but he couldn't pull his beak out.

Pedro began to slide down the length of the sail.

Then BUMP! Pedro landed on the deck.

As he fell backwards, his beak became detached from the sail and the sail split in two. *Swallow* ground to a halt and the scarlet macaw fell off his perch into the sea. Pamela squawked admiringly, swooped down from the top of the mast and gave Pedro a peck on the cheek. Pedro turned bright pink, picked himself up and led Pamela off towards the sunset. He didn't even look back.

For a moment we were all so gobsmacked we forgot to keep racing. *Sally*'s sails began to flap wildly as we bobbed alongside the Swiggers' motionless ship.

Samantha Swigger stared at her sail in disbelief then started complaining by shouting furiously across the waves to Dame Kittiwake.

'No rules broken!' replied Dame Kittiwake. 'Carry on!'

Samantha Swigger stared hopelessly at Hornswaggle Rock. It glittered in the sun, so close yet so far.

'No rules broken?' came a loud voice from across the sea behind us. 'What absolute rot!'

I spun round and spotted the smart white catamaran hurtling towards us at top speed. For the first time we were close enough to spot a small woman on board. She had shiny brown hair and she was wearing a smart pair of jeans, a yellow oilskin coat and a red life jacket. She looked a bit familiar.

'What on *earth* makes you think someone can get away with vandalising their fellow competitor's sail?' she continued.

'Where I come from, CHEATING is SIMPLY NOT ON!'

I giggled and turned to the others, expecting them to laugh too.

But Arabella and George weren't laughing. They looked completely and utterly gobsmacked.

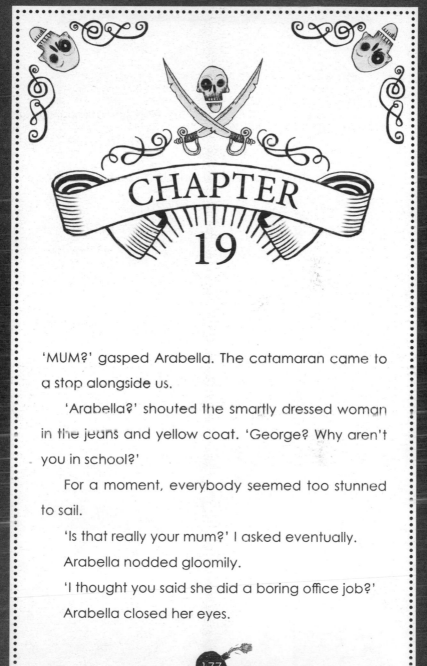

CHAPTER 19

'MUM?' gasped Arabella. The catamaran came to a stop alongside us.

'Arabella?' shouted the smartly dressed woman in the jeans and yellow coat. 'George? Why aren't you in school?'

For a moment, everybody seemed too stunned to sail.

'Is that really your mum?' I asked eventually.

Arabella nodded gloomily.

'I thought you said she did a boring office job?'

Arabella closed her eyes.

'She does.'

'Then what's she doing out here in the Hornswaggle Boat Race?'

Arabella let out a cross sigh.

'I haven't the first sniff of an idea,' she said. 'But one thing's for sure, I'm going to find out.'

'Mum,' she shouted across the churning channel of water between our two boats. 'You're meant to be at work. What are you doing here?'

The woman in the yellow coat tilted her head to one side and folded her arms across her lifejacket.

'I *am* at work,' she said, sounding just like Arabella.

'We're on our office team-building day. And I must
say, it's jolly good fun.'

'Mum,' groaned Arabella, shaking her head.
'There's nothing jolly or fun about
this, you're in the middle
of a pirate boat race.'

'Darling!' laughed
Arabella's mum.
'You are a hoot.'
She blew kisses
to her children.
'We're having a
super time!' she
said. 'Aren't we?'

The rest of her crew
looked really seasick.

'If only I'd known you were competing in it with your school,' she said cheerfully. 'I could have come with you instead. I could have been one of those – what do you call them, oh yes, parent volunteers. I must tell Dad to remind me about these things.'

'Mum,' said Arabella through gritted teeth. 'We're not on a school trip. We're in the Hornswaggle Boat Race and that woman bearing down on you is Samantha Swigger, A.K.A. Captain Swigger, A.K.A. leader of the famous Cornish pirate crew, A.K.A. reigning champion of the Hornswaggle Boat Race. Now that her own boat is damaged, she's not going to stop until she's hijacked someone else's – in other words, yours!' Arabella paused.

But Arabella's mum was cleaning her glasses.

'Mum!' shrieked Arabella, as Samantha Swigger got out a large oar and started paddling *Swallow* towards the white catamaran. 'Watch out!'

'Do you mean to say,' frowned her mum, 'that you're on unauthorised leave from school? That means you won't get the hundred-per-cent attendance certificate this year? You've had it every year since pre-school. Oh heavens, we might even get a fine. And who are these scruffy-looking children you're with? I don't like the look of them at all. And more to the point . . . YOU'RE NOT EVEN WEARING LIFE JACKETS.'

Arabella rolled her eyes.

'On the other hand,' continued their mum. 'I suppose *if* you win, this will be excellent for your CVs. We don't have to mention this rabble.'

Maud scowled.

'I'll bite your bottom with my tooths,' she said. 'I'll bite it really, really hard.'

'Teeth,' hissed Arabella. 'For the seventy hundredth billionth time, you say *teeth* not tooths.'

Maud cackled.

Arabella closed her eyes and took a deep breath.

'Mum, I'm serious,' she said, pointing at the Swiggers. 'Any minute now these people are going to board your boat and they'll either make you walk the plank or feed you to the sharks.'

'Oooh is that part of the package? I'll ask.'

Arabella and George's mum smiled brightly and shouted over the wind at Samantha Swigger.

'Sorry to bother,' she said. 'But are extras like walking the plank included in the original price? If not, we don't mind paying a bit more. We're a FTSE-100 company, we're given a very healthy budget for our office team-building days. Do you prefer cheque or credit card?'

Swallow was now just a few metres from the catamaran. Samantha Swigger pointed her oar at Arabella's mum.

'Hand over your ship or the whippersnappers cop it,' she said without blinking. Members of her crew were getting ready to jump aboard.

'Good heavens!' shouted Arabella and George's mum. 'This race is FULL of cheats.'

Samantha Swigger flung down the oar and tried to lasso the white catamaran with a long rope.

Her crew threw daggers, attempting to puncture our own sails.

'Mum!' yelled Arabella. 'You've got to get out of here before they board your boat!'

George ducked to avoid a small dagger and tightened *Sixpoint Sally*'s mainsail.

'Well honestly!' shouted their mum from behind us. 'They didn't say anything about pretending to be pirates when I booked!'

'Bert, Maud!' I shouted. 'Look out!'

Bert and Maud ducked to avoid a cutlass.

'Heave ho!' puffed Arabella, pulling up the genoa. *Sixpoint Sally* pulled away from the other boats just as Samantha Swigger was getting ready to jump aboard the catamaran.

'What fun!' shouted Arabella and George's mum, hoisting the catamaran's sails and yanking on the ship's wheel.

'Noooooooo!' roared Samantha Swigger. 'They're getting away.'

'Have you had a cool drink? Have you had enough to eat?' called Arabella and George's mum across the water. She was alongside us again.

'Ignore her,' muttered Bert, not taking his eyes off the chequered flag on top of Hornswaggle Rock. 'Push *Sally* harder. We can't let her beat us.'

'Young man,' she said crossly (sounding quite like Arabella). 'If you're going to be rude to me, please don't refer to me as *her*. I'm not the cat's mother. My name is . . .'

I pushed *Sixpoint Sally* ever so slightly starboard. Wind filled her mainsail, giving us a bit more speed. We edged ahead.

'. . . Cecelia!' she shouted.

Bert and I burst out laughing.

Arabella and George grinned apologetically. Once they'd got over the shock of finding out that their own mother was competing against us in the Hornswaggle Boat Race, they'd been really embarrassed. I could see why. Anyone with a decent pair of sea legs could see that Cecelia wasn't normal. Mums are meant to be crazy and shouty and wild. Mums don't fuss about whether you've had enough to drink.

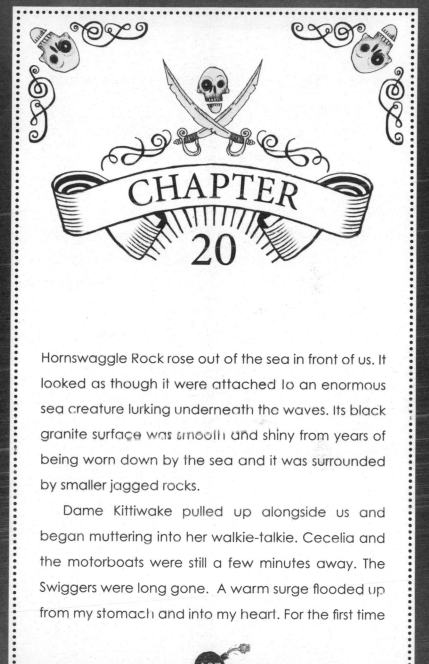

CHAPTER

20

Hornswaggle Rock rose out of the sea in front of us. It looked as though it were attached to an enormous sea creature lurking underneath the waves. Its black granite surface was smooth and shiny from years of being worn down by the sea and it was surrounded by smaller jagged rocks.

Dame Kittiwake pulled up alongside us and began muttering into her walkie-talkie. Cecelia and the motorboats were still a few minutes away. The Swiggers were long gone. A warm surge flooded up from my stomach and into my heart. For the first time all day, I began to believe that we might actually win the race.

'Blimey!' gasped Bert. 'Hornswaggle Rock is way bigger than I remember!'

'I can't get *Sally* any closer,' I said. 'Not with all those other rocks.'

The sea was rising fast. At high tide, Hornswaggle would be submerged by water again – and the chequered flag would disappear with it. We didn't have long. If I wanted to reach that flag first, I was going to have to swim. I grabbed Bert and handed him the Blighty Bling. I blocked out the battering of the wind and the roar of engines from the approaching motorboats.

I dived in.

The water was icy cold. One of my feet brushed against something long and slimy. For a few minutes, all I could hear was the plunging sound of my hands, the *gung-gung* beat of my heart and the gentle crash of water breaking over Hornswaggle Rock.

The chatter from the boats behind me got fainter. My toes kept catching on sharp bits of rock.

My mouth and nose filled with water. My chest ached. I understood why Mum had put us through those weeks of training.

When my hands finally hit something hard and flat, I lifted up my head and took huge, gasping lungfuls of air. I turned to wave at the others. But to my surprise they didn't wave back. Nor did any of the spectators.

'Vic!' shouted Arabella. 'Watch out!'

A strange noise echoed through the air.

It was getting closer.

I turned round. Flying out of Shipwreck Strait towards me was a kitesurfer. He wore tight red swimming trunks and diamond earrings. His hair was jet-black. There is only one person on the planet with hair that black.

Captain Guillemot the Third.

I had no idea how he'd managed to catch up with us but I knew he would do anything to reach the flag before I did.

'Don't look up,' I told myself. 'Just climb.'

This was easier said than done. The sides of Hornswaggle Rock were wet. Plus, there were barely any nooks and crannies to support my hands and feet.

Guillemot was a swirl of colour as he sped towards me.

'Vic!' screamed Bert. 'Hurry!'

I dug in my fingernails and tried to remember what Mum had said during our climbing training sessions. She'd yelled things like, 'Grip with your knees and pull with your arms.' She'd shouted, 'If it doesn't hurt you're not doing it properly.' She'd told us to hurry up.

But no matter how hard I tried to follow Mum's instructions, I wasn't quick enough.

I was only halfway up the rock when Guillemot pulled up alongside me.

'Need a hand?' he said, flashing his gold teeth. 'Shall a proper pirate show the ickle McScurvy how you REALLY win the famous Hornswaggle Boat Race?'

Hornswaggle Rock was now surrounded by *Sixpoint Sally*, the white catamaran and Dame Kittiwake's speedboat. Just behind were the television crew and spectators. They began to chant.

Guillemot pushed me off the rock into the sea.

'Unsporting!' shouted a spectator from the largest motorboat.

'Eliminate him!' said a journalist.

'No rules broken!' replied Dame Kittiwake. 'Kitesurfs and dastardly behaviour are permitted. Carry on!'

There was a murmur of disapproval from the crowd. Then silence. Guillemot laughed nastily.

'I'll show you how to win the Hornswaggle,' he

said, launching himself up the rock. 'I'll show you how a real pirate does it.'

Guillemot got ready to climb further. He tried to pull himself up with his hands and . . .

. . . he slipped.

The crowd sniggered. For the next thirty seconds, Guillemot floundered in the water at the base of the rock. No matter how hard he tried, he couldn't climb it. I swam further round the rock and pulled myself back up.

'Buzz off, you barnacle!' said Guillemot. 'The only person who's going to climb this thing is ME!'

'An exciting finish is taking place out here at Hornswaggle Rock,' reported a TV journalist. 'It's a David and Goliath battle for the flag. Will the young pretender outwit the famous muscleman?'

The side of the rock was sheer and I had to keep avoiding Guillemot's kicks.

'I'm lodging a complaint!' Guillemot spluttered, sliding down again. 'This rock is too slippery.'

'Complaint dismissed,' snapped Dame Kittiwake from her boat. 'Hornswaggle Rock was checked three times at low tide this morning. It is in perfect working order.'

'Here here!' cheered Cecelia, trying (and failing) to steer her catamaran closer to the rock (she obviously didn't realise that the only way to reach it was to swim). 'A good workman (or workwoman of course) never blames his (or her) tools. That's what I always tell my children. Don't I, Arabella?'

But Arabella wasn't listening.

'It isn't the rock that's slippery,' she announced,

194

smiling. 'It's him! All those beauty treatments have made his skin so smooth and soft, he can't climb any more. He's lost his grip – literally!'

Journalists scribbled in their notebooks and the crowd roared with laughter.

'Shut UP, ginger nut!' snapped Guillemot. 'Anyway, who said I needed to climb the stupid rock? I'll just wait for the McScurvy brat to come back down. I have this.'

Guillemot pulled out an enormous ruby-encrusted cutlass. The flag was now close enough for me to touch. I shut my eyes and stretched up my hand as far as it would go. I felt my fingers brush against the soft silk of the flag. I pulled.

'I've got it!' I shouted at the top of my voice. 'I've got the flag!'

For a few floating seconds I was so happy I forgot to hang on to the rock.

Big mistake.

CHAPTER 21

'Gotcha!'

Guillemot's arms closed around me as I fell on top of him. Up close, he smelled of rotten fish and strong aftershave. I held my breath and prayed. I didn't want to die. I wanted to explore the world with the Treasurescope. I wanted to find Mum and tell her we'd won the Hornswaggle Boat Race. I wanted to stay up all night eating ice cream.

'Hand it over!' Guillemot raged, trying to pull the flag out of my fist. His fingers slipped again.

'You see!' shouted Arabella. 'He's lost his grip!'

We both staggered to our feet and Guillemot jabbed his cutlass at me. The blade was so sharp I could almost hear it squeaking. He put his mouth to my ear.

'If you don't give me that flag!' he whispered. 'I'll cut your hand clean off.'

This was what Dad would call a lose-lose situation. Not even Mum would be laughing right now. I didn't want to lose my hand. For one thing, pirate hooks don't come in children's sizes.

'Hand it over!' This time it wasn't Guillemot speaking. It was Arabella. 'Don't be a fool,' she said. 'Not even the Hornswaggle is worth losing a hand for.'

'She's right, Vic,' called Bert grimly. 'Let him have it.'

George held up his fist encouragingly.

Cecelia, on the other hand, turned the colour of cherry cola.

'Let him have it?' she said. 'You can't just *give up*. Don't be intimidated by the opposition, my girl. Learn to hold your nerve.'

The spectators stopped chanting. I tightened my hand around the flag. Cecelia was right. McScurvys didn't give up.

'We won that flag fair and square,' I told Guillemot through gritted teeth.

'Nothing fair about the Hornswaggle Boat Race,'

he laughed nastily. 'You know that, I know that, even my old pal ginger nut knows that. Hurry up, will you, I've got a massage booked for 4 p.m.'

I felt the blade of Guillemot's cutlass press down on the soft skin of my wrist.

'No!' I said. 'I'll never hand over this flag. Never! You'll have to slice my hand off first.'

'That's my girl!' cheered Cecelia. 'Now you're behaving like a real pirate!'

Dame Kittiwake picked up her walkie-talkie and spoke into it.

'Send the ambulance boat out to Hornswaggle Rock,' she said. 'And tell them to step on it.'

Guillemot smirked and pressed his cutlass down on my wrist. At first I just felt a weird tingling sensation as he sliced into my skin. The real pain came a few seconds later. It felt boiling and freezing at the same time. It felt like the end – except it didn't end, it went on and on and on. I saw my own blood dripping into the bluey-grey water.

A terrible moaning scream filled the air. This must be what dying sounds like, I thought. I looked down at my hand, expecting to see a bleeding gap where it had been. But the hand was still there.

Even more surprising, it was still holding the flag. The scream wasn't coming from me, it was coming from Guillemot.

'Aaaghghhghghghl'

'She bit me!' he roared, clamping his hands to his bottom and dropping his cutlass. 'That baby bit me on my bum!'

There was a loud cackle from below and I looked down to see two big brown eyes staring up at me.

'Maud!' I gasped.

'I'm teeving!' she said happily. 'It's my tooths.'

'Teeth!' shouted Arabella from *Sixpoint Sally*. 'Teeth not tooths!'

I crammed the flag into my T-shirt and wriggled out of Guillemot's grip.

'Thanks, Maudie,' I shouted, grabbing my sister's hand and leaping off the rock. 'Now swim! Swim for your life!'

Maud and I set off like a pair of flying fish.

'He's behind you!' screamed Bert. 'He's catching up.'

'Yes,' spat Guillemot. 'And you're not getting away from me this time.'

My wrist throbbed where Guillemot had cut into it. My lungs were bursting and everything seemed to hurt. We were now alongside *Sixpoint Sally*. Maud reached the ladder first. I watched as George hauled her out of the sea and handed her a strawberry sherbet. I heard the familiar crunching sound as Maud bit down on it.

'Come on,' I told myself. 'Just a few more strokes.'

I felt a tremor pass through the water next to my feet and inhaled a fishy stench.

Guillemot was right behind me now.

'Don't worry, Vic!' shouted Arabella, leaning over the side of *Sixpoint Sally* and dipping her hat into the water. 'I'll give the old goat a dumping.'

Arabella threw a hatful of water over the side of the boat. It landed slap bang on top of Guillemot.

'HOW DARE YOU?!' screamed Guillemot. 'I'M NOT SUPPOSED TO GET MY HAIR WET FOR AT LEAST TWENTY-FOUR HOURS.'

'It's about time a smelly old soak like you had a shower,' Arabella told Guillemot, sounding pleased with herself. 'Have another rinse!' And she chucked another hatful of water over the side.

Black dye began to pour down Guillemot's face.

'She's blinded me!' he shouted. 'I can't see a thing.

I . . .' But I didn't wait to hear what he said next. I swam to *Sixpoint Sally*, pulled myself up the ladder and collapsed in a drippy heap. The warm wood of the deck had never felt so welcome. I let out great gasps of relief.

'Well,' said Arabella, smiling down at me and showing me her dripping hat. 'Thank goodness for the costume department.'

'I thought you weren't supposed to damage school property,' I croaked.

Arabella grinned, wrapping a piece of old cloth around the cut on my wrist.

'Dastardly times,' she said, 'call for dastardly measures.'

I grinned back at her and lifted the flag.

'Besides,' said Arabella briskly, 'if I get it dry-cleaned at the weekend, no one need ever know.'

CHAPTER

22

We set off for Shabbers-on-Sea. Television cameras flashed as we sailed past. Flares and fireworks exploded in the air. Music played on a loudspeaker. Boats honked their foghorns. Television crews raced over in speedboats.

Dame Kittiwake spoke into her walkie-talkie.

'The McScurvys have won,' she said. 'Yes, I was surprised too. Yes, they are rather a motley bunch. That's right, they're on their way back for the prize-giving.' She nodded. 'But you'll need to send a boat out here to rescue Guillemot. He's floating out to sea on a piece of driftwood. Yes, that's right – Captain Guillemot the Third. And, just to warn you, you may have trouble recognising him. His hair isn't black any more, it's . . .' Dame Kittiwake paused, '*it's grey.*'

The sky turned blue, white and pink. The twinkling turquoise sea filled with marshmallowy foam. A family of dolphins leaped alongside us as we sailed on. Maud shared out the last of her strawberry sherbets, Bert elbowed me in the ear, George grinned and Arabella held up the flag.

The Swiggers booed as we whizzed past. The O'Drearys threw soggy iced buns (and missed). The Rattle-Dazzlers sped over to us in their speedboat and shouted rude words.

I couldn't even smile. Winning the Hornswaggle Boat Race was the most amazing thing that had ever happened to us but with Mum and Dad still missing there was nothing to celebrate.

The journey home took longer than expected. The wind was against us and the tide was on the turn. It seemed to take hours. By the time we reached the bay of Shabbers-on-Sea the sky was turning mauve.

'Arabella, George!' hollered Cecelia, who was STILL alongside us. 'I think yachting might be your best sport yet. Do you want to start sailing lessons? We could fit them in on a Saturday morning, between your private tutor and county swimming?'

Arabella didn't bother replying.

'Talking of county swimming,' Cecelia continued, 'I think we might just make training this evening. But you can always invite your piratey friends over for a play date next weekend.'

'Mum,' hissed Arabella. Her voice was carried across the water by the wind. 'Pirates sail the seas and search for treasure. They don't go on play dates.'

But Cecelia wasn't listening. She was too busy looking through her binoculars.

'What a funny-looking vessel!' she said. 'I've never seen a boat like that out in the middle of the sea. Surely it should be tied up safely in a canal somewhere. It doesn't look very seaworthy. Look at all that peeling yellow paint. Look at the rust. There's even a hideous old telly in the middle of the deck. Oh and what a strange . . .'

Bert and I didn't wait to hear what she said next. We raced to the front of *Sixpoint Sally* and peered at an ancient yellow houseboat that was motoring towards us. Steering it was an old lady with bright blue hair. She was wearing dungarees, a stripy T-shirt and she was carrying a knobbly walking stick topped with a silver toucan. We didn't need a telescope to tell us who she was.

'Granny McScurvy!' shouted Bert. 'Ahoy there!'

Granny McScurvy waved her walking stick.

'I got your message,' she hollered, pointing at
Pedro who was sitting on the end of the tiller with a
wing round Pamela. 'He turned up a few hours ago –
in the nick of time. I picked up your mum and dad in
the Bay of Barnacles. They were about to be sucked
into a whirlpool.'

She pointed in front of her. There, sprawled on the
deck of the houseboat, eyes glued to the enormous
telly, was a tall, muscly woman in a bright pink, short-
sleeved party dress and a small scruffy man with
a beard and an upside-down mouth. They were
soaking wet and covered in seaweed.

'Mum!' we shouted. 'Dad!'

Our parents leaped up and rubbed their eyes.

'Shiver me timbers,' whooped Mum. 'They're
alive!'

Dad wiped his forehead with relief.

'It was your mother's fault for crashing out and
not setting an alarm,' he grumbled.

'Ooooh,' laughed Mum. 'Someone's in a grump!'

I could tell they were about to start one of their
fights so I held up the flag. For a moment there was

silence. Then Mum picked Dad up and danced round the deck, holding him above her head. Dad cried and waved his cutlass in the air. Granny McScurvy got out her guitar and played a rock shanty at top volume. They stamped and cheered and yelled.

'We've won!' Mum shouted at Dad. 'We've finally won the Hornswaggle Boat Race! And it's all thanks to our brave whippersnappers!'

'*Excuse me!*' interrupted Cecelia from the deck of her catamaran. 'But your whippersnappers would never have won without Arabella and George helping them. Besides, with all the cheating I witnessed, I'm not sure that anyone deserves to win – not if we're telling the absolute truth and playing by the rules.'

Arabella let out a long sigh.

'Oh, Mum,' she said. 'For the LAST time, these people are pirates. Telling lies and breaking the rules is what they *do*. And sometimes,' she went on in a slow, quiet, careful voice, 'it's what George and I do too.'

Cecelia stared at Arabella with her mouth open.

'Darling,' she gasped at Arabella, shaking her head and tutting. 'I'm going to pretend I didn't hear that.'

Cecelia was still tutting when we sailed into Shabbers-on-Sea. We tied *Sixpoint Sally* to the harbour wall and waved at the large crowd that had gathered on the jetty. Dame Kittiwake pulled up alongside us, climbed aboard *Sixpoint Sally* and handed us the winning trophy.

The crowd erupted.

We took it in turns to hold the famous Treasurescope. Engraved all over it, in tiny swirly writing, were the names of previous winners – there were Swiggers and Kittiwakes, Guillemots, Rattle-Dazzlers, O'Drearys. We even found our grandfather Stan McScurvy's name, faded and worn, from 1984. And there, at the very bottom, were some new names, freshly engraved.

Vic Parrot McScurvy

Bert Parrot McScurvy

Maud Parrot McScurvy

Arabella Ursula Brooke-Taylor

George Sebastian Brooke-Taylor

I ran my finger over our names and felt something fizz like sherbet within my chest. But it wasn't until I looked through the Treasurescope's lens that I realised what we had really won. There, at the end of the lens, was a three-dimensional map of an island. The view of the island was so detailed that it was almost as if I was looking at it for real. There were palm trees, swamps, hidden caves and . . . red crosses. You don't have to be a pirate to know what red crosses on an old map mean.

'Treasure,' I gasped. 'Loads of treasure.'

I twisted the Treasurescope's lens to the left. The island I'd been looking at vanished and another map appeared in its place. I twisted the lens again . . . and the same thing happened. Every time I turned the lens, I found myself looking at a new treasure map.

The fizzy feeling in my chest spread to my arms and legs and up to my head. I felt a bit like I might explode. I lifted the Treasurescope in the air one last time and let the roar of the crowd flow around me like warm syrup.

A long time later, after we'd posed for photographs and signed autographs and stuffed ourselves with too many chips, it started to get dark.

The crowds headed home and our parents crashed out in their bunk beds. Even Cecelia nodded off on the bridge.

But we didn't go to bed. We followed Granny McScurvy into the moonlit town and played arcade games . . .

. . . all night long. **The End**